T0336317

starfall

Starfall

A TRIPTYCH

Lars Kleberg

Translated from the Swedish
by Anselm Hollo

Hydra Books
Northwestern University Press
EVANSTON, ILLINOIS

Hydra Books
Northwestern University Press
Evanston, Illinois 60208-4210

Printed in the United States of America

ISBN 0-8101-1454-2

Library of Congress Cataloging-in-Publication Data

Kleberg, Lars, 1941-
  [Stjärnfall. English]
  Starfall : a triptych / Lars Kleberg ; translated from the Swedish by
  Anselm Hollo.
    p. cm.
  ISBN 0-8101-1454-2 (alk. paper)
  1. Imaginary conversations. 2. Eisenstein, Sergei, 1898-1948—Fiction.
  I. Hollo, Anselm. II. Title.
  PT9876.21.L37S7513   1997
  839.73'74—dc21   97-41968
                                                            CIP

The paper used in this publication meets the minimum requirements of the
American National Standard for Information Sciences—Permanence of
Paper for Printed Library Materials, ANSI Z39.48-1984.

Contents

The Aquarians

The train from Berlin to Moscow rolls through the night. A Soviet first-class compartment: red plush upholstery, antimacassars, reading lamps with bead-fringed shades, mirrors above the seats. The compartment is littered with cardboard boxes, suitcases, Mexican blankets, books. A human skull sits on one of the hat racks. Through the glass doors, and behind the window on the other side of the corridor, lights, freight cars, etc. can be seen flashing by. EISENSTEIN *reclines in a corner of the compartment, wrapped in a soft overcoat cut along the lines of a bathrobe, his hat pulled down low over his eyes, apparently asleep with a book in his lap. The door opens.* BRECHT *enters in a sports jacket, no tie, a leather cap on his head, and an extinguished cigar butt between his fingers.*

BRECHT   Doctor Eisenstein, I presume? [EISENSTEIN *does not react. After a pause:*] Doctor Eisenstein, I presume?

EISENSTEIN   [*Does not react. Pause. Turns a page of the book. Another pause.*] Wait. [*Goes on reading, makes notes in the margin.*] Forgive me, I'm in the sixteenth century. [*Makes notes.*] You've never been there, I shouldn't think. [*Suddenly closes the book, sits up straight, pushes his hat back.*] But of course. You're going to Rome, too. The third Rome. [*Chuckles. Then, in an obliging tone:*] Have a seat, there's plenty of room.

BRECHT   [*Sits down.*] These Russian carriages are really solid. Just like in the good old days.

EISENSTEIN   I only wish it wasn't so damned cold. I hope you packed enough warm clothing. However—as I just read here—in the sixteenth century, indoor temperatures were no higher than fifty to fifty-nine degrees. Only once in a while people would

3

light a proper fire in the fireplace. [*Pause.*] Have you been to the Soviet Union?

BRECHT No, I'm sorry to say I haven't. But—as they say—I've seen the movie! Honestly, your films have increased German interest in the Soviets tremendously.

EISENSTEIN That's always nice to hear.

BRECHT Speaking of such, do you know if our friend Tretyakov is in Moscow just now?

EISENSTEIN I have no idea. I'm sure you know more about what goes on in Moscow than I do.

BRECHT Tretyakov was in Berlin last year. We discussed his play *I Want to Have a Child.* There were interesting analogies between it and our film *Kuhle Wampe,* which we'll be showing in Moscow. [EISENSTEIN *closes his eyes.*] In terms of the model concept, to be more precise. Both Tretyakov and I agreed—in opposition to the bourgeois aesthetic of "entering into the spirit of things"—that works of art should be designed as models, analogous to those used in science. I hope I'll be able to discuss these ideas with other Soviet colleagues when we get to Moscow.

EISENSTEIN [*Looks up.*] You really believe that stuff? It sounds like a chemistry lesson. Chemistry without the magic.

BRECHT [*Lights his cigar butt.*] When you get a chance to see our experiment, *Kuhle Wampe,* you'll—

EISENSTEIN [*Brusquely.*] I've already seen it. And that's exactly what is wrong with it. *Man merkt die Absicht.*

BRECHT I don't think you've seen the entire film. It was butchered by the censors. Unfortunately, we haven't met with any comprehension in our Party press, either. We could use your and your comrades' criticism and support for our continued work. [EISENSTEIN *smiles, produces a big can of Mexican candies in the shapes of small skulls, bones, phalluses, toads, snakes, etc., all coated in powdered sugar. Offers them to* BRECHT, *who declines. Picks out a candy toad, licks it with relish, puts it in his mouth, takes it out again, sucks on it before chewing and swallowing it.*] In our day, reality can only be shown as a *quotation.* Even in the theater, it is incredibly difficult to show those quotation marks; but on film, paradoxically enough, it seems to be even harder. The technique itself has to be put between quotes. But the resistance to our experiments is the best indication that we are on the right track. When we wanted to try a bit of ironic sound montage, the firm that monopolizes sound technology in Germany refused to cooperate. They said it was impossible, it would damage their equipment; all of a sudden they were unable to record the sound, and so on. It was not *permitted* to liberate the technology! To wake up the audience!

EISENSTEIN   That's quite a story. But surely a rejection of il-lustrative sound does not mean that the technology has to be used at some kind of . . . distance? That would be completely undialec-tical. Sheer vegetarianism! No, as Loyola says, the end sanctifies the means. [*Chuckles.*] You know what? The only artistic experi-ments that interest me today are the ones in which Joyce has—

BRECHT   Yes, right, but that is exactly—

EISENSTEIN   [*Suddenly emphatic.*] —Joyce has shown the way— that is to say, where the experiment itself is identical with the work, where every chapter is also a study—

BRECHT   [*Interrupts.*] Yes, and where every part could indeed be produced by different subjects, so that the montage cancels out the work's traditional—

EISENSTEIN   [*Stubbornly.*] No, not at all! Where every part is also a study, a parody, and it does not cancel but *includes* earlier, more primitive forms on a new level. In that way, the text becomes a cross section of an entire consciousness with all its strata, just as in our interior discourse, where we can move with lightning speed, and unconsciously, from one level to the next. *That* is where Joyce's genius manifests itself in his interior monologue, not in his, or that woman's, whatever her name is, who sits and takes a shit— we don't give a shit for the contents of his or her thoughts—no: what is genius is his *vertical montage,* in which one can swing like a monkey between the most regressive and the most advanced in the same second, the same frame. If I ever get to finish my Mexican film, you'll see what I mean. It won't be anything like your and Tretyakov's chemistry lessons. It is boring to discuss the *how* versus the *what.* The only important thing is the question of the *effect.*

BRECHT   That is precisely the question we Marxists are trying to ask; at least, I hope so.

EISENSTEIN   The only problem is how to achieve the greatest possible effect. I remember how, even when I first showed *Potemkin* in Berlin in 1926, there were some young comrades who berated me for its being too pathetic. But the pathos is exactly what makes it effective! All our later attempts to make an intellectual film have only aimed at a better *control* of pathos. To compel even a bourgeois audience to become incensed over the cruelty of tyranny and to cheer the triumph of solidarity—that becomes possible only when you are in command of the art's organic laws, of the structure of pathos. Once you have discovered that secret, you can really make gold!

BRECHT   Gold? I don't doubt it. [*Pause.*] But there are several things here that seem unclear to me. First of all, are you saying that the viewer should sympathize with the revolution without understanding why? Second, the capitalist's enthusiasm over solidarity's triumph is likely to cool down as soon as he leaves the cinema—or at the latest the following morning, when he discovers that the workers at his factory have gone on strike. But, okay, the bourgeois's capacity for art appreciation may just be unassailable. And third, and this is the most serious problem, the petit-bourgeois or worker who sees your film may feel like a revolutionary while he is in the cinema, but later on he won't realize how unemployment turns him into a fascist. Your pathetic method transports him, from the reality that has to be mastered, to a world of revolutionary illusions, a new "Potemkin village," as it were, decked out with a red pennant. I admit that I was moved by your film when I saw it, but it did not convert me to Marxism.

EISENSTEIN   [*Smiles, picks out a piece of candy shaped like a snake.*] Is that the German criterion for revolutionary art?

BRECHT   [*Tries again to light his cigar butt.*] We aim to turn the audience into an accomplice, not into a victim—not even a victim of revolutionary emotions. No, into accomplices who join the producer in destroying the aura that surrounds the medium and, indirectly, reality itself. This is a process fraught with suspense—though not of the kind Aristotle recommends. When all is said and done, it is a matter of creating a form the Fascists cannot adopt and use for their purposes.

EISENSTEIN   But that is sheer vegetarianism! Surely one does not have to force oneself to hop along on one leg just because some people don't know how to walk properly? I have spent more than a year in Mexico, and I am now convinced that it is best to walk on both legs, never mind that this is a terribly ancient method. The most striking things about Mexico are not the contrasts but the way the old and the new interweave and present themselves in one and the same thing—in one and the same person. In the peon's unfathomable dark eyes you can read a thousand years of humiliation. The way children seek the shade, the way women carry children on their backs, these preserve the memory of the past; every gesture is charged with sensuousness and history at the same time, and there is something both completely animalistic and completely rational in the way they move. [*Pause.*]

I have also tried my luck with the capitalist film industry. In Hollywood. It was, of course, quite impossible to work there. But then I was given the opportunity to be an independent producer—or so I believed. Like an idiot. [*To himself:*] It may have been a trap. [*Louder:*] Mexico. Not a film about Mexico, but a film with Mexico, across Mexico, in the spirit of Mexico. Nowhere else have I ever sensed such possibilities for making a film in which the progressive and the regressive would function together, where the most modern, most differentiated and cerebral would join the prelogical, protoanimal, vertebral aspects of our consciousness. The director in the fetal position, the director as a fish. [*Chuckles.*] In the very method of the film. Joyce's interior monologue multiplied into an enormous tragicomical chorus, in which death's triumph simultaneously is the hour of resurrection—

BRECHT   [*After a pause during which he searches his pockets for matches and finally manages to light his cigar again.*] I don't quite understand. What was the *new* thing you wanted to show in your film?

EISENSTEIN   The old. The carnival—surely you, as a Bavarian, know about that? Pregnant Death, the King's death and resurrection, the Lord of Misrule, the world turned upside down, man turning into woman, woman into man, the child becoming king, the fool becoming wise. *Re-volu-tion* in the most literal sense of the word. But not the cyclical as such—that time is gone—but the perennially returning traumatic transition from the cyclical to the linear, and back from the linear to the cyclical. The trauma of the fish when it left the sea. The trauma of birth. To make one's way back to the water, over and over again, and to be thrown back onto dry land again—or to throw oneself onto dry land, once one has learned one's lesson. [*Pause.*] Now I'm lying here again, panting. Just as I was getting close to my objective, they killed the project. [*Hums.*] "All of me, why not take all of me?" [*Pause.*] They say it was Upton Sinclair and that sow with all the money. But no, it was on orders from Rome. You can quote me on that. [*With sudden clarity:*] No, don't do that. [*Chuckles.*] No, you see, it was because I was getting close to uncovering their secret. I was about to succeed where no one else had. [*Pause.*] Behind them stands the Inquisition. [*In a whisper:*] Do you hear me? I fear for my life. [*More or less to himself:*] Maybe I should have gone with that Spanish marquis instead.

The little devils took everything away from me, and told me they'd send the footage to me as soon as I got back home. After the project has been approved, I can go there again and finish the film. Ha. Just as you think you are free to *do it,* he sneaks up on you. The shadow. Il Commendatore. The dead hand. [*Sings, with a small but clear voice:*]

All of me, why not take all of me?
Can't you see, I'm no good without you?
Take my lips, I want to lose them,
Take my arms, I'll never use them.

Your good-bye left me with eyes that cry,
How can I go on, dear, without you?
You took the part that once was my heart,
So why not take all of me?

[*Pause.*] Do you know who wrote that? Marks. Gerald Marks. It was in one of the new musical films I saw just before I left. [*Pause.*] They'll always take your best. [*Pause.*]

All of me, why not take all of me?
Can't you see, I'm no good without you?
Take my lips, I want to lose them,
Take my arms, I'll never use them.

Your good-bye left me with eyes that cry,
How can I go on, dear, without you?
You took the best, so why not take the rest?
Baby, take all of me!

Do you know why they took away my film? I was onto their secret. But they were mistaken: the secret is not in the footage. I have it right here. [*Points with his left hand to the right side of his head.*] So I'll just have to start over. Tabula rasa. Clear the decks. [*Picks a small skeleton from the candy tin.*]

BRECHT   [*After a pause.*] You haven't thought about emigrating?

EISENSTEIN   I don't think you should ask anyone that question when you're on your way to Moscow. By the way, who is that woman with you, the one with the hair in a bun? Is she your— guardian angel? [*Whispers:*] Watch out for her. Don't tell her what we've been talking about. [*A little too loudly:*] No other country has the production resources I need.

BRECHT   Does the Soviet Union have them?

EISENSTEIN   Not yet.

BRECHT   So you really think the Five-Year Plan will guarantee the production of your film?

EISENSTEIN   Wouldn't you take that chance? Emigrate. The stars don't care if you do. [*Pause.*] We are pretty different, aren't we? My name is alchemical: Eisen-stein. Yours is mechanical: Brecht, the one who breaks.

BRECHT   No, that would be "Bricht."

EISENSTEIN   Brecht, Hecht, Knecht, Recht. What a language. You don't believe in that, in *nomina sunt omina?* You don't believe in omens? And you are going to Moscow!

BRECHT   I'm not going there out of an interest in superstition. Rather the contrary.

EISENSTEIN   Then I must warn you. What you call superstition has experienced an enormous revival since the revolution. Just take a look at Lenin's mausoleum when you get there. The dead prince mummified. It's the old Egyptian magic that has made a comeback. The mausoleum itself is a pyramidal structure, with just a bit of the top sliced off. With a balustrade, behind which the high priests can make their calculations and the military commanders receive the salutes of their forces. It is really a reconstruction of the Tower of Babel. Even though the best Soviet contribution to that genre was Tatlin's tower—but they never built it, sadly enough.

BRECHT   But what in Pharaoh's name does Tatlin's constructivism have to do with magic? [*Contemplates the skull on the hat rack.*]

EISENSTEIN   Don't be so sure it doesn't. Tatlin's tower was designed to move in unison with the heavenly bodies—the base completing a full turn in a year, the middle part in a month, and the top once every twenty-four hours. Its height was 398 meters; that's a well-known magical number. And I have heard that sun worship à la ancient Egypt is now all the rage in Moscow. But it was really Lenin who charted the course for all of that. Did you know that Campanella's *The Sun State* was one of his favorites? A utopian republic, governed entirely according to the laws of astrology. Not to mention the Red Star: it is the Pythagorean pentagram, the symbol for the alchemists' magical stone. So there you are. Red magic. [*Chuckles.*] Well, I'm sure you've read *Faust*. It'll help you draw your own conclusions, once we get there. [*The train brakes suddenly, and the skull—which turns out to be a Mexican artifact made out of sugar for the Day of the Dead celebration—tumbles from the hat rack and shatters on the floor.* EISENSTEIN *quickly gets down on his hands and knees and picks up paper scrolls and small pamphlets that were hidden inside the skull. He kicks the pieces of the skull under the seat and hastily stuffs the papers in his coat pocket.*]

BRECHT   Magic seems to be the new thing all over the world. A few weeks ago, a French film crew came to Berlin, and one of their actors tried to convince our sound technicians that they could record spirit voices if they ran the tape at triple speed. I had seen the guy before, by the way. He was there when Pabst made his miserable hodgepodge of *The Threepenny Opera*. Specializes in Jesuits and poisoners.

EISENSTEIN   What a coincidence! I met that crazy man, too. His name is Artaud, right? Antonin Artaud. One of the truly great. He convinced me that we are, all of us, hopelessly timid and lukewarm. I was supposed to give an interview, you see, about the future of film and so on, and I had agreed to meet this lady journalist at a restaurant. So I was sitting there, explaining all the mysteries of the art to her—who knows what she made of it all— and then he suddenly stood there, the madman, as handsome as a figure by El Greco, all aflame. He proceeded to take over the entire interview, explaining that film was dead, that it belonged to a bygone era, being merely an afterbirth of the nineteenth century. The upshot is that he scared off the cow-eyed lady and we were left with the tab. But he knew how to skip that, too. Back there in Paris, he seems to be living off bread crusts and morphine, in some kind of surreal coterie of fakirs and magicians. And, yes, he had written a manifesto for *the alchemical theater*— that's what he called it. I have it right here, just a minute, I'll read you some of it. [*Pulls a pamphlet from his coat pocket.*]

BRECHT   Was he also peddling tracts on Halley's Comet and sexual abstinence? Those types are beginning to be as common as the Nazis' street patrols. For all I know, they may be working for the same bosses. [*Lights the cigar stub.*]

EISENSTEIN   Don't be so sure of that. Listen to this: [*Reads.*] "There is a secret correlation between the fundamental principles of the theater and the alchemical arts. When one examines the nature of the theater and its foundations, one finds that it, just like alchemy, builds upon a certain number of fundamental principles, and in the realm of the imagination these are as effective as those that *actually* transmute base matter into gold in the physical sphere. Alchemy with its system of signs can be seen as the spiritual double of an action that concerns only actual matter. In the same way, the theater should also be seen as a double—not of immediate reality but of another, more dangerous, archetypal reality, in which Primal Forms emerge like dolphins only to disappear just as quickly into the dark deeps."

BRECHT   Isn't it remarkable how these modern mystics have lost control even of their language?

EISENSTEIN   But listen to the content. It is as scientific as your, and Tretyakov's, models. It's just that it's a question of . . . another science. Listen to this: "The Eleusinian Mysteries resolved the oppositions between spirit and matter, idea and form, abstract and concrete, and consolidated all outward appearance into an expression that must have resembled distilled gold." Nevertheless, we can't find our way back to the mysteries. Today, he said, only *shock* can capture an audience. "Metaphysics can reach our senses only in the most violent manner—*through our skins.*" The theater of cruelty, he called it, a theater that would be like a devastating plague.

BRECHT   A plague?

EISENSTEIN   In a certain way, this is the most consistent application of our theory of effect, much more logical than behaviorism, or pathos, or whatever. He has made an in-depth study of oriental theater, he has been initiated into the mysteries, and he is convinced that the only sure way to reach an audience is by means of cruelty.

BRECHT   But that's sheer obscurantism!

EISENSTEIN   Oh, no, he has progressed from there. The obscure, the darkness is only the initial stage, you see: the *nigredo*—it is the first stage of the alchemical process. Chaos, unconsciousness, the primal darkness. It is followed by the *albedo,* the white stage, which is purification, separation of elements, conscious dualism. That's just about where you are now. [*Chuckles.*] Then comes the highest stage—the red, *rubedo.* Right! That's where red magic comes into play. Believe an old man's words: magic has excellent prospects.

BRECHT   Old? You're no older than I am.

EISENSTEIN   Yes, I am. When were you born?

BRECHT   Ninety-eight.

EISENSTEIN   What a coincidence. What day and month?

BRECHT   What difference does that make?

EISENSTEIN   It always makes a difference.

BRECHT   February tenth.

EISENSTEIN   [*Turns pale.*] February tenth? Oh, my god. And you don't believe in omens! Meyerhold was born on February tenth.

Pushkin died on February tenth, after the duel. And on February tenth a catastrophe will occur in my life. [*Pause.*] So you are an Aquarius, just like me. I was born on January twenty-second, 1898.

BRECHT   So?

EISENSTEIN   The sign of Aquarius. Haven't you heard about it? [BRECHT *shrugs.*] Aquarians are searchers; they love contradictions, inventions, revolution, carnival, utopianism, avant-gardism—everything under the influence of Uranus. Their favorite flower—the narcissus. [*Picks a phallus out of the candy tin, sucks on it, stares at* BRECHT, *takes the candy out of his mouth again.*] Very interested in extravagant eroticism and astrology. You just haven't discovered that yet. [*Chuckles.*] It is curious that our paths should cross just now, at the age of Christ, 33⅓ years, Dante's *mezzo cammin,* you know. The greatest dangers lie in wait for us when we try to accomplish something before the time is ripe, to drive across the bridge before it has been finished. You see, we are constructors, architects: the arts are our field of experimentation—Lewis Carroll, Mozart, Thomas More, Byron, Copernicus, Giordano Bruno, Galileo, Lorenzo di Pupo, Francis Bacon . . . Swedenborg and Strindberg—probably the only two Swedish Aquarians. But also Edison, Darwin, Charles Lindbergh. And now you. It all fits.

BRECHT   Right, and then there's our new rising star in politics, little Adolf the house painter. Surely he belongs to that group. A true avant-gardist, in his own way. No, the only thing we have in common is that we're born in January or February. Pure circular reasoning! *Idem per idem.* It doesn't say anything that's *new.*

EISENSTEIN   You, too, are a lover of books—although you prefer to steal them rather than to buy them, isn't that so? [*Laughs.*] The tenth of February. A certain penchant for perfidy or indolence, a man of fighting words, fond of intrigues, but not particularly courageous when the chips are down, oh no. Great disappointments and captivity. I am the twenty-second, that's Kabbalah; you're the tenth, that's the decimal system. Although that's really Kabbalah, too. Just wait and see. [*Stuffs the entire phallus in his mouth, chews.*]

BRECHT   What do you have in that tin? Cocaine? [EISENSTEIN *makes a deprecating gesture.*] A friend of mine has told me a great deal about the effects of hashish on visual perception. "The artificial paradises," "the devil's elixirs"—isn't that right up your alley?

EISENSTEIN   No, no. I'm interested in quite different . . . means.

BRECHT   But seriously now: there is something that disturbs me in the news I get from Moscow, and from Tretyakov's letters. The scientific wing of Marxism seems to be losing ground to the ideological, to the new priesthood, to all those things you call magic. "Engineers of the human soul"—what the hell is that supposed to mean? Those who abolished "souls" in the name of reason are now trying to inoculate them into masses who can no longer rely on their own intelligence? And not without success, it seems. But that is unacceptable—surely you agree. An ideology that, instead of forcing people to *see through* events, exhorts them to genuflect before the incomprehensible! This must be exposed before it is too late. Otherwise, the masses both here and over there are left more perplexed than ever.

EISENSTEIN   We must talk more about that once we get to Moscow. [*Pulls a couple of thin scrolls from his coat pocket. A pause.*] Frankly, there is only one thing about you that I approve of: you really do believe in what you say. All cardinals are atheists. All politicians are apolitical. You'll never become one of them. [*Opens the door to the corridor, looks out, closes the door again. In a hurried whisper:*] Here is something I would like you to carry across the border. I'm sure you understand. [*Puts the papers in* BRECHT's *hand.* BRECHT *looks at the little scrolls with distaste.* EISENSTEIN *whispering:*] Hide them, fast. Anywhere. But not in that cap. [BRECHT *pushes the scrolls into the top of one of his thick wool socks.* EISENSTEIN *picks up the book. In a voice that seems a little too loud:*] Maybe you're wondering why I talk so much about Rome and the church? It is this story of Giordano Bruno of Nola, the runaway monk, that I can't get out of my mind. The one who was burned at the stake. He denied not only that the earth was the center of the universe, replacing it with the sun—just as that Polish fellow Copernicus did. No, the man from Nola said *there was no center!* No wonder the Inquisition grabbed him. Science has never been as revolutionary before or since, and the Great Art was never as central to things as then. Giordano wanted to create an alternative church, or an alternative party, or perhaps even an alternative world. But the prelates said that there was only *one* world, the only permissible one, in which the earth was in the center and Rome was the center of the earth. As the sun revolved around the earth, the cardinals revolved around the pope, and the people around the priests, and the laborers around their masters, and the wife around her husband. How else could it possibly be? When Giordano said—

BRECHT   "On the contrary!"

EISENSTEIN   No, he said more than that. He said, "There is no center here, we are in the universe and the universe is in us, and our world is only one of infinitely many possible worlds." And that was considered scandalous. I think it would be considered just as scandalous today.

BRECHT   What a coincidence! I, too, have been interested in that period. Copernicus's *De revolutionibus* was truly revolutionary science. Bruno, Galileo, Bacon—all of them questioned everything, tested everything in practical terms. They liberated science from Aristotle's and the Scholastics' clutches. Superstition had to give way to reason, chemistry was divorced from alchemy, astronomy from astrology, art from worship. [*Pause.*] I think we should collaborate on something about Bruno. A performance in Moscow. I'll write it, you'll translate it. And we can both direct it.

EISENSTEIN   You and I? About Giordano Bruno? In Moscow? In that case, it would have to be an opera. [*Suddenly the light in the compartment goes out. Only the blue emergency light remains on. A long pause during which only train noise is heard. The light comes on again.* BRECHT *checks to see that the papers are still in his sock.*] Opera is the only form in which one could possibly present such incendiary material. Tragedy and buffoonery in the same breath. Bruno's life and work provides material for both.

BRECHT   Today opera exists only as a parody of itself. Both of my efforts in the genre—*The Threepenny Opera* and *Mahagonny*— attack the genre itself.

EISENSTEIN   Precisely! And the more you parody it, the more it remains itself. I have seriously considered using Wagner in my new film on Kreuger, the Match King. *Götterdämmerung*—stock market crash accompanied by Wagner's trombones of destruction. But that's another story. Giordano Bruno does belong to opera, for several reasons. First of all, they are contemporaries. Opera was invented at the end of the sixteenth century by a few Florentines who thought they could recreate Greek tragedy. They came up with a form for a kind of alchemical wedding of elements: words, music, images, dance. And that wedding was the subject of practically all their operas: the trials, the purification, and the union of the protagonists, all through the power of music.

BRECHT   Is there a planetarium in Moscow?

EISENSTEIN   Yes, and it's a brand-new one.

BRECHT   Can one put on performances there?

EISENSTEIN   Yes, yes, that's brilliant! Under the round vault of the dome—better than old Vitruvius! The theater, a universe, and the universe, a theater! Everything joined together, as the circuit closes in a magnetic magic circle: the hero, the chorus, the orchestra, the audience. And here we perform the story of the great magician's rise and fall. Magnificent! I'll talk about it with an old friend who works at the planetarium—as soon as we get there.

BRECHT   [*Lights the butt.*] But the joining of elements can only take place in the prolongation of their separation—thus against the background of their separation. One could hardly demonstrate the break with Aristotle by means of some kind of Wagnerian *Gesamtkunstwerk* in which everything dissolves into everything else, like a gourmet smorgasbord on the high seas. I think that the planetarium can be seen as a model for a way of seeing that differs from the old theater. In the Aristotelian thèater the viewer is taken for a ride, as if on a merry-go-round: he believes that it is he who is urging the wooden horse to run faster, he who steers the little boat. The new type of theater we are working with is much more like that planetarium: the viewer observes the connections critically and enjoys his overview. In the merry-go-round model the viewer is active, but only within the fiction. In the planetarium model he is passive, but only for the time being, within the walls of the theater. Like the new science of our day, a piece on Giordano Bruno must draw boundaries where none existed before, it must differentiate in order to be accessible. No tautologies, but questions. The chorus narrates, the hero demonstrates, the music comments. The diverse elements are made accessible to the viewer in the same way that the world was mastered by means of the astronomers' and mathematicians' measurements.

EISENSTEIN   Mastered, yes, but—measurements? Are we talking about the same thing? Giordano never saw a telescope! His critique of the divine Aristotle was revolutionary, but his was not the only one. The truly subversive thing was his own teaching. He was a disciple of the great Hermes Trismegistus. He believed that he could master the elements by means of the Great Art, the *Ars Magna*. His fate was sealed as soon as others believed that they could steal his secret. For Giordano, the universe was a boundless work of art, written in a secret language. "You can be the master of the universe, just be sure not to stroke it widdershins." A mystical joker, a jocular mystic. "Pedants have their clocks, we mathematicians have our laughter" was another one of his sayings. Listen to this; it is about the unity of opposites. [*Reads from the book.*] "Twofold are the numbers, odd and even, feminine and masculine. Twofold are the desires, high and divine, low and vulgar. There are two roads of life, *cognitio* and *affectio.* Twofold are their objectives, the true and the good. Twofold are motions, the straight ones, by means of which bodies strive toward their maintenance, and the circular ones, by means of which they are maintained. Twofold are the fundamental principles of things, matter and form. Twofold are the qualities of substances, sparse and dense, simple and complex. Twofold are the opposing active principles, heat and cold. Twofold are the sources of nature: the sun and the earth."

[*The compartment door slides open. The train noise becomes intense, the curtains flutter in the breeze. Both men look at the door, motionless. After a long pause, the door closes again, as if moved by an invisible hand.*]

BRECHT   [*Checks the papers in his sock, then takes the book from* EISENSTEIN.] Such power! Such prose! [*Reads, becoming progressively*

more hesitant.] "See, here is he who has traversed the air, pene-
trated the sky, scanned the constellations, crossed the boundaries
of the world, burst the alleged walls of the first, eighth, ninth, and
tenth crystal bowl, and everything else attached thereto by the
tricks of simpleminded mathematicians and the blind fancies of
dime-a-dozen philosophers. Led by the light of sense and reason,
with the key of tireless research, he has opened the gates of truth
for us all [*glances at the compartment door*] and has shown hidden
and veiled nature naked; he has given eyes to moles and the
returned their sight to the blind." [*Lights the cigar butt.*] Who did
this fellow from Nola think he really was?

EISENSTEIN   He believed that he was holding the *Magna Clavis,*
the Great Key to the Universe, in his hand.

BRECHT   And to whom was he going to give it? To the people?
Or to a new caste of priests?

EISENSTEIN   If one were to use the Inquisition's interrogation
protocols as a framework—which would be a simple but effective
theatrical solution—his encounter with Galileo would be an important scene. Did you know that Galileo beat Giordano in their
competition for the chair of mathematics at the University of
Padua in 1592? The young mechanic was chosen over the polymath magician in a typical academic intrigue involving bribes
and all those kinds of things. Not that Giordano was all that good
at arithmetic. In any case, he now realized that this was his last
chance after seventeen itinerant years that had made him famous
and notorious all over Europe. His friend Lorenzo di Pupo, who
had spent some time in Moscow, tried to console him with that
old Russian proverb—how to translate it?—"What never happens
is best," or "What happens is best"—it goes both ways. Giordano
was actually ready to go to Moscow to become Boris Godunov's
court astrologer, but Lorenzo advised him against it. Unfortunately, the alternative, Venice, proved to be no better. After a
couple of months, the Inquisition arrested him. And modern
physics ended up in a blind alley. The scenes in the cellar of Sant'
Officio should turn out to be very . . . attractive. During the seven
years the man from Nola was imprisoned in Rome, he was sub-

jected to practically every known method of torture—with the exception of crucifixion. In addition to such well-known numbers as the lead-lined chamber and the red-hot tongs, there are descriptions of *il polledro*, "the foal," in which the victim is stretched by means of ropes across a pyramid-shaped set of steps; *la corda*, being hoisted up by a rope; and finally *la veglia*, "the wake," in which the victim's body was pressed against a sharp wooden edge for thirty-six hours while his limbs were twisted out of their sockets. *That* could be a theater of cruelty to shut up even a Moscow audience!

BRECHT   [*After a pause.*] But what did you mean by "blind alley"?

EISENSTEIN   Galileo's victory over Bruno meant the beginning of the triumphal progress of the mechanists. If you look at it that way, it was no coincidence that Giordano was condemned to be burned at the stake on Galileo's birthday. Who knows, maybe it was the tenth of February. [*Chuckles.*] Then things just went on like that—two times two equals four, two times two equals four, two times two equals four. And the further along that went, the more soulless the universe became, and so did the science about it. But while nature has become soulless, it also has become more and more inaccessible. The part of nature that *won't* fit into the mechanistic and positivist straitjacket has grown larger and larger. Today, Galileo is our Aristotle! While the physicists have a lot to learn from that laughing madman Giordano. He said that his opponents' way of describing the universe resembled someone who, when asked to give an account of a book he has read, proceeds to describe its format, the kind of paper used, the number of pages, and the typography, but never gets around to the book's content. Doesn't that sound familiar? As Giordano told his judges before he was tied to the stake, "Our dialogue continues in eternity."

BRECHT   But Bruno's doctrine of infinity turned out to be historically nonproductive! You can't say that about Galileo's mechanics. Bruno's ecstasy over the infinite may just have been the obverse of his fear of the finite, when he was faced with the chance, and necessity, to try to master the elements in a practical manner, instead of just invoking them. In which case he does seem quite disturbingly modern. There are quite a few who have started making gold according to his prescription.

EISENSTEIN   Are you saying that the alchemists only invoke reality, instead of affecting it the way the mechanists do? Why, then, are you so afraid of what you regard as empty invocations? Surely you aren't *superstitious?* [BRECHT *tries to light the cigar butt.*] Today quantum mechanics tells us that there may be an infinite number of possible worlds alongside the one we are now observing. Every second something happens here, the opposite occurs alongside of us, in another world. Every alternative event then generates its possible extensions, so that the universe may well be an infinitely branching tree of possible and simultaneously existing worlds. Which can be neither proved nor disproved. And so, in another world, next door, you are me, and I am you. [*With lightning speed,* EISENSTEIN *grabs* BRECHT*'s cap and replaces it with his own hat, which is several sizes too large for* BRECHT. *Imitating* BRECHT*'s voice:*] Now then, Dr. Eisenstein, if you are such a great sorcerer, how about conjuring us some supper? It's about time. Only vegetarian, of course. Culinary enjoyment is a distraction. I prefer eating with pointers for chopsticks.

BRECHT   [*Imitates* EISENSTEIN, *takes the candy tin.*] In the meantime, just try one of these Mexican magic bullets—they can make you travel through both time and space. Or have a taste of this one. [*Picks out a phallic figure.*] If this one's too small, I can find a bigger one. [*Sings falsetto:*] "All of me, why not take all of me?"

EISENSTEIN   No thanks, I prefer one of these . . . feet. [*Takes a piece of candy.*] No rule without an exception. You see, I don't favor the smorgasbord, but I do enjoy gnawing on a fellow human if he has flesh on his bones and marrow to suck.

BRECHT   Umm. . . . Regression, regression! Ah, to feel one hasn't forgotten one's old tricks, to swish one's tail. Speaking of such, did you know that they found the remains of Bruno's tail in his ashes on Campo di Fiori? Oh, to have been there, to see him go up in a glory of fire, whispering his last curses against science and progress! What wouldn't I give to have been there, to smell the odor of burnt flesh, to jostle among the ecstatic crowd, to dissolve in it, to feel all boundaries melt away? [*The train slows down. In a normal tone of voice:*] This must be the border. [*Red flags can be seen passing the window.*]

EISENSTEIN   [*Still in* BRECHT's *tone of voice.*] The problem with Giordano was that he claimed there was no center. If that is so, no one can tell front from back. How, then, can one know what is progress? Your poor Giordano was unable to solve that problem. And that's why he won't do as a subject. Bye now. [*Gets up.* BRECHT *gets up too, grabs his cap, tosses the hat on the seat, and rushes out.* EISENSTEIN *calls out, in his normal voice:*] Remember what Giordano said: "Our dialogue continues in eternity!"

[*The train has stopped; the view through the window on the other side of the corridor is obscured by steam.* EISENSTEIN *sits down again, pulls his hat down over his eyes, resumes his initial pose.*]

The Sorcerer's Apprentices

Proceedings of a meeting held in Moscow on 14 April 1935, on the occasion of Mei Lan-fang's, the Chinese actor's, visit to the Soviet Union.

SPEAKERS
(in the order of their appearance)

NEMIROVICH–DANCHENKO, VLADIMIR IVANOVICH,
theater manager

TRETYAKOV, SERGEI MIKHAILOVICH,
playwright, reporter

STANISLAVSKI, KONSTANTIN SERGEYEVICH,
stage director

MEYERHOLD, VSYEVOLOD EMILYEVICH,
stage director, theater manager

TAIROV, ALEKSANDR YAKOVLEVICH,
stage director, theater manager

EISENSTEIN, SERGEI MIKHAILOVICH,
film director

CRAIG, GORDON,
British theater theoretician

PISCATOR, ERWIN,
German stage director in exile

BRECHT, BERTOLT,
German playwright in exile

SJÖBERG, ALF,
Swedish stage director

KERZHENTSEV, PLATON MIKHAILOVICH,
Party member, expert on cultural matters

Moscow, 14 April 1935. The meeting hall in the quarters of VOKS, the All-Union Society for Cultural Connections with Foreign Countries. The red stage curtain has been decorated with large black-and-white portraits of Lenin and Stalin and two garlands of the world's flags, attached at the top to the middle of the upper edge of the curtain and descending symmetrically to the sides. On either side of this arrangement hang the flags of the Soviet Union and the Republic of China.

On the stage stands a long table covered with green felt, behind which are seated, from the left (as seen by the audience): VOKS Chairman AROSEV; *Chairman for the evening's discussion, manager of Moscow's Artistic Theater* VLADIMIR NEMIROVICH-DANCHENKO; *playwright* SERGEI TRETYAKOV; *and* PLATON KERZHENTSEV *representing the State Committee for Artistic Matters. To the right of the table stands a lectern.*

The audience consists of a select number of Soviet theater people, actors, cultural workers, scholars, and a few foreign guests. Somewhere in the front row sits the evening's guest of honor, the Chinese actor MEI LAN-FANG.

The audience settles down, grows quiet.

NEMIROVICH-DANCHENKO   Honorable Dr. Mei Lan-fang! Comrade Chairman of VOKS! Colleagues!

The unforgettable guest performance given by Dr. Mei Lan-fang's theater, and the response it has received, testify to the great friendship of the peoples of the Soviet Union and China. China's and Russia's former rivalry is now a closed chapter, after the victory of our great October Revolution, and after China's decision to choose the path of anticolonial revolution. Today we can say with certainty that our great countries will only grow closer and closer to each other in the years to come. [*Applause*]

The art of Chinese theater has met with the greatest interest from the Soviet public. Dr. Mei Lan-fang's masterful appearances, and his private demonstrations and discussions with colleagues, have—as I can personally testify—proved extraordinarily stimulating, at least from the Soviet point of view. Today our country, with its multinational character, is particularly qualified to understand and appreciate this art, one which has truly "shaken the world."

The encounter with China's theater seems especially important today, as we workers of the theater reexamine our traditional practice in the light of socialist realist theory. Its importance may not yet be entirely clear to all of us. But one thing is certain: it defends realism against various decadent strains whose connection to the Fascist contagion is obvious. This can only be welcomed with satisfaction by all progressive Russian artists who have dedicated themselves to Pushkin's dictum: "*Fidelity to reality remains the condition and foundation of dramatic art*"!

In the hope that tonight's discussion about the Chinese theater will proceed in the spirit of humanism and realism, I now give you our playwright Sergei Tretyakov, a great friend and connoisseur of China, and one of the initiators of Dr. Mei Lan-fang's successfully completed visit. [*Applause.*]

TRETYAKOV Comrades! Dr. Mei Lan-fang's visit has affected the Soviet public and the Soviet theater workers like a Chinese New Year's fireworks display: we are dazzled and dazed. A dramatic art long surrounded by a wall of ignorance and misunderstanding has shown itself to us, here, in all its uncompromising clarity and collective discipline. We have much to learn from this theater, both as performers and as audiences. We thank Dr. Mei Lan-fang for giving us an opportunity to attend, if only for a short while, his severe academy.

The Chinese theater has been received with unqualified enthusiasm by both the Soviet public and our theater's own cadres. Now that the demonstration is over, we must ask the question,

What has been the basis for this enthusiasm? I do not want to exclude the possibility that it has been partly due to misunderstanding. Especially today, whether it is a question of politics or art, general enthusiasm is anything but satisfactory. We must also know *why* we are enthusiastic. Allow me to point out a few aspects of the Chinese theater's mode of functioning that are quite remote from our general practice.

First of all, the Chinese theater is not an elite theater for an isolated Mandarin clique, or for people specializing in aesthetic pleasures. It is a theater for an entire people, of a kind long dreamed about in the West, one that can be realized today, but not unconditionally, by the construction of socialism.

The Chinese theater is a traditional people's theater, still an important part of Chinese life, on workdays and holidays alike. The repertoire is the same for the thousands of theaters in China's towns, and it is loved and understood by all levels of society, from sweaty coolies to ministers and professors wearing starched European collars. This theater has a far-reaching social function, comparable only to the influence the Christian church has had, and modern advertising now has, in the West.

Theater in China is a mouthpiece for the country's ancient, feudal, authoritarian ethics. Loyalty and obedience are the favored themes of its plays: the son's obedience to his father, the subject's to the emperor, the wife's to her husband, the student's to his teacher, the servant's to his master. Representatives of virtue are rewarded just as surely as evildoers are punished—in this life or one to come. The obligatory resolutions of Chinese plays remind one of other dramatic forms with strictly standardized endings: classical tragedy (the implacability of fate), Christian liturgy (the triumph of the divine principle), or American film (the victory of efficiency and profit).

The Chinese theater is, in effect, a theater of agitation, and its primary characteristic is the conscious targeting of its expressive moments at the psyche of the audience. It is not mimetic. It *works on* the viewer by visual and acoustic means.

VOICE FROM THE AUDIENCE   Are you talking about art or about agitprop?!

TRETYAKOV   I am speaking about art that has an agitative function, something that has existed in all historical times. But let me
get to my next point.

Second: while perhaps only 5 percent of all Chinese have
mastered the written symbols of their language, there is no doubt
that 95 percent understand the symbols of the stage. The pro-
foundly traditional language of that stage guarantees its popular
accessibility, and, at the same time, its ideological effect. Every
Chinese person knows, or will learn, that, for example, if an actor
has a white spot on his forehead, this means that he is a villain, but
that if the spot is red, he is a good person. The audience expects
signs, symbols, and masks with strictly defined meanings.

Since ancient times, all female roles in the Chinese theater
have been played by men, even though there now are some all-
female theater groups in southern China, the less tradition-bound
part of the country. Nevertheless, audiences still mostly prefer to
see male actors in the female roles. Dr. Mei Lan-fang's own example is, of course, most revealing in this respect. What the Chinese audience wants to see on stage is not *a* female, but *femininity,*
that is, signs that stand for femininity.

Third: the Chinese theater is not merely a powerful engine for
ideological formation. In fact, today's audiences, who know the
pieces by heart, are not engaged so much by the ethical propaganda as by the way it is presented: by the actors' gestures, by their
superior acrobatics—in sum, by the *technical* aspect of the artistic
work.

This is so because the Chinese theater, apart from its mission
to hypnotize the audience to absorb its feudal ethics, does serve
the masses in another way. As a foreigner with some familiarity
with this theater, one soon recognizes the gestural patterns and
intonations of the stage in every conversation between two Chinese persons, in every street scene with its masterfully rehearsed
bows, greetings, steps, and hand gestures. Chinese theater is a
kind of school of behavior, a powerful institution for the stan-
dardization of the forms of everyday life and emotional life!

Comrades and colleagues!

As a people's theater, the Chinese theater has no rivals. Its audience consists not only of five hundred million Chinese but also of three hundred million inhabitants of adjoining countries—a total of half the population of the planet. For this reason alone we greet Dr. Mei Lan-fang and his troupe with the most profound respect. But we do so for yet another reason: the determined and uncompromising work of our guests is a model for a people's theater for the other half of humanity. The Chinese theater, which will one day be liberated from the shackles of feudal ideology, bears the promise of a rational and international theater, a theater that by exact methods rouses and leads the disciplined masses in the struggle for a new and beautiful world! [*Applause, hubbub.*]

NEMIROVICH-DANCHENKO We thank Comrade Tretyakov for his "factographic" and engaged introduction. While it has left unanswered certain questions regarding realism in the Chinese theater, this may well provide a starting point for lively discussion. Quite logically, but first and foremost due to the privilege of age and wisdom, we will now ask the master of realistic Russian stagecraft to open our conversation. I give you the people's artist, Konstantin Sergeyevich Stanislavski! [*Prolonged applause.* STANISLAVSKI *makes his way to the lectern with some difficulty.*]

STANISLAVSKI Colleagues! For me, this encounter with Dr. Mei Lan-fang's theater has been a both unsettling and vivifying [*coughs heavily*] encounter with great art, Theater with a capital *T.* On our own stages what we see only too frequently is merely routine, craft, theater with a lower-case *t.* This is true regardless of which school the actors in question believe they represent.

Not without sadness in my heart, I have to say that this is true even of certain adherents—indeed, perhaps the most militant adherents in particular—of the so-called Stanislavski method. Their puffed-up soulfulness has as little to do with true dramatic art as cockfights in Oriental markets. [*Laughter, scattered applause.*]

But let me, instead, say something about the Theater with a capital *T* with which Dr. Mei Lan-fang has entranced us in a series of unforgettable performances. The experience has been enhanced by the fact that the art that has conquered us comes from a foreign culture. Allow me to remind you of a passage in

Lev Nikolayevich Tolstoy's profound and still not fully understood essay *What Is Art?* Tolstoy points out that while a speech made in Chinese will remain incomprehensible to me unless I have a command of the Chinese language, I can be moved and "infected"—that is the word Tolstoy uses—"infected" by a Chinese work of art. "What distinguishes art from every other kind of psychic activity is that its language can be understood by everybody, and that it infects everybody without exception. A Chinese person's tears or laughter infect me just as much as a Russian's; the same thing happens with a Chinese painting, or music, or poetry, if the poem has been translated into a language I can read." I am certain that if Lev Nikolayevich had known Dr. Mei Lan-fang, he would have added Chinese theater to his list, in spite of his well-known skepticism regarding the stage.

What our guests have made us experience, first and foremost, is that *great art reaches all human beings,* without exception. They have also demonstrated that the human being, despite all differences of class, language, and race, is surprisingly and reassuringly homogeneous—that he is the person to whom all art pays homage. "The hu-man be-ing! That is splendid! That sounds . . . proud! The hu-man be-ing!" It was my privilege to speak those words for the first time in 1902, at the inaugural performance of Maxim Gorky's great play *The Lower Depths,* and I spoke them thereafter over three hundred times. Each and every time they sounded new, while their profound message remained the same.

However, a human being is not a human being unless he also *wants to become* something greater than what he *is.* The highest form of human self-realization is found in art, and primarily in the art of theater. To show the innermost nature of the human being, to clarify and make it come alive for one and all—therein lies the task of our art.

When Dr. Mei Lan-fang, with incomparable grace, opens an invisible door or suddenly turns to face an invisible adversary, he makes us see not only that motion but the action itself, *the targeted action*. This Chinese demonstration has once again convinced me that all who are genuinely interested in the essence of the actor's art find their common ground in this: *Not the motion but the action, not the word but thè utterance.* Therefore, I was not surprised but confirmed in my belief in the universality of the laws of art when Dr. Mei Lan-fang, master of rhythmic motion and exquisite gesture, in a conversation with me emphasized *psychological truth* as the alpha and omega of the actor's art. Dr. Mei said that the Chinese actor's art can be perfected only by means of practice and empathy, and went on to state a principle we have, indeed, also discovered, even though we arrived at it by entirely different routes: "The actor must feel himself to be the heroine he is acting; he must forget that he is an actor; he must, as it were, merge with the character." [*Coughs heavily.*]

I thank Dr. Mei Lan-fang for letting me see, in my lifetime, yet another one of the great realistic actors, comparable in his mastery to a Salvini or a Yermolova. [*Thunderous applause.*]

NEMIROVICH-DANCHENKO   Our next speaker is the director of the National Meyerhold Theater, the people's artist Vsyevolod Emilyevich Meyerhold. Welcome! [MEYERHOLD *mounts the stage vigorously. On his way there, he squeezes* STANISLAVSKI*'s arm with a quick but cordial gesture.*]

MEYERHOLD   The significance of Dr. Mei Lan-fang's visit is much greater than any of us can even guess at today. Just now we are merely astonished and enchanted. But after our Chinese guests have gone home, we who are the creators of the new theater in this country will be affected by their influence as if by a delayed depth charge. Our theater is preparing to restage one of my old presentations, Griboyev's *The Curse of Genius.* But when I went to rehearsals after having seen a couple of Dr. Mei Lan-fang's performances, I knew that everything had to be redone from the ground up.

In his introductory remarks, Nemirovich quoted Pushkin's words about fidelity to reality being the foundation of all dramatic art. However, he did not allow Pushkin to make his final point. In his article about people's theater, the poet goes on to say, "But what if the true nature of theatrical art is the improbable?"

Ever since Pushkin's time, two tendencies have struggled to dominate Russian theater: one of them led us into the cul-de-sac of naturalism, and the other has proven fertile only in recent times. It is no accident that Pushkin's greatest plays still haven't been staged, or that the attempts to do so have been discouraging. Imagine *Boris Godunov* staged according to Dr. Mei Lan-fang's methods! That would be a journey through the poet's marvelous tableaux, without any missteps into the marsh of naturalism that sucks everything into its mire.

I would really like to talk about all the positive and joyful things this Chinese visit has given us, but that would take hours. Let me restrict myself to two points.

In recent times, there has been much talk here about the significance of facial expression and motion, about the interplay between word and motion. But we have forgotten the most important thing, and Dr. Mei Lan-fang has now reminded us of it: to wit, *the hands.*

Frankly, comrades—when you do the rounds of our theaters after having seen his performances, you will agree with me: we might as well cut off all our actors' hands, since they do not seem to have any use for them! Let us chop off these hands that stick out of their cuffs but do not express anything at all, that don't say anything, or else say something else than what they should be saying!

VOICE FROM THE AUDIENCE   How can you say that about your own colleagues? There are enough other people who would like to chop off our hands! [*Boos, hubbub.*]

MEYERHOLD   If you don't want to hear the truth, just use your hands to close your ears. [*Laughter, applause.*] So, the hands—that was my first point. My second point concerns rhythm, tempo, and motion. We are fond of speaking about the rhythmic construction of a performance. But anyone who has seen Mei Lan-fang's theater must recognize how incredibly backward we are compared to these geniuses of the stage.

There is nothing in our performances—whether of opera or drama—that forces the actor to subordinate himself to *scenic time.* We have no feeling for time. We don't know what it means to have an economy of time. The Chinese count in tenths of a second, we count in minutes. One might as well remove all the second hands from our watches—they are completely superfluous!

Comrades! I believe that the Chinese theater's significance for our Soviet stage will be enormous. In twenty-five or thirty years we may witness a synthesis of these different experiences. Then we may see our inheritance from Pushkin realized to its fullest extent, in a manner of which Dr. Mei Lan-fang has given us a foretaste. The theater of the future will no longer be a theater of the *probable,* but a theater in which realism and imagination are joined in a new way, in a heightened realism, a socialist realism! [*Applause.*]

NEMIROVICH-DANCHENKO   We thank Vsyevolod Emilyevich for his vigorous, very personal words. Our next speaker is the people's artist, stage director at our National Chamber Theater, Aleksandr Yakovlevich Tairov. [TAIROV *proceeds to the lectern in a possibly even more vigorous manner than* MEYERHOLD.]

TAIROV   To all who have eyes to see and ears to hear, Mei Lan-fang's unique theater has shown that theater is and will always be *art.* Any attempt to subordinate the theater to some other authority, be it enlightenment, religion, or political agitation, is misguided and diverts the theater from what it is and has to be: *theater!* Only if it is allowed to be just that—emotion, beauty, rhythm—it can also serve people in our great socialist homeland.

The Chinese theater has demonstrated this since time immemorial, and I am proud to be the first among all Russian stage directors to have learned from it. As early on as in my Moscow production of the Chinese play *The Yellow Blouse* at the Free Theater, in 1913, I made use of the classical Chinese theater's forms in an effort to get away both from dreary naturalism and misanthropic symbolist mysticism. The coordinated forms and colors, the harmonious ensemble of bodies and voices—that was exactly what we wanted to give the Russian masses, even before the revolution, encouraged by the Chinese people's theater's example. Ever since that time, the Chamber Theater has charted the course between the Scylla of naturalism and the Charybdis of ideological force-feeding—in Dr. Mei Lan-fang's spirit, even though we did not know his name then. Now we are proud to have welcomed Dr. Mei Lan-fang in our midst, and we will always regard him as the first and foremost honorary member of our ensemble! I want to repeat the words inscribed on the pillars framing the classical Chinese theater stage: "May you play well for a hundred years!" [*Applause.*]

MEYERHOLD   [*Rushes up to the lectern.*] Comrade Chairman! I must ask your permission to object to such patently incorrect historiography. While arguments about chronological priorities in artistic matters lack dignity, I must nevertheless remind everyone of the *generally known* fact that, in 1910, Meyerhold's "intermedia house" was the first stage in Russia to employ the principles of oriental theater.

Furthermore, Tairov's comments show, once again, that he has never understood the significance of *movement* in the theater. Oriental theater attaches extraordinary importance to movement. When we consider movement we often think of the ballet and of mime. There are theaters that have developed their style from balletic movement, such as, indeed, the Chamber Theater. But the Chinese theater shows us something very different from this decorative halfway house between ballet and theater. The Chinese theater's movements are grounded in realism. All of its movements derive from folk dance—from a culture in which a dancer as well as someone who carries a yoke with buckets of water or a sack of rice down the street regards his movements as *dance movements,* not as predetermined ballet steps but as something founded on a certain rhythm. There is as much dance in these movements as there is rhythm in dance. The Chamber Theater insists on regarding movement as something *decorative*— and this has led to the futility of its pedagogical experiments and the eclecticism of its productions.

TAIROV   [*From his seat in the audience*.] And what, dear Vsyevolod Emilyevich, happens to movement in your biomechanical system? You transform the theater into a cruel machine in which the actors become soulless cogs, and the poet's words become mere drive belts in the machine! Where does the feeling go—the thing that makes us gather on either side of the footlights?

NEMIROVICH-DANCHENKO   Colleagues, I must insist that you adhere to our agreed order of speakers! Our next speaker is the commendable art worker, director of Soyuz Kino, teacher of film direction at VGIK, Sergei Mikhailovich Eisenstein, whose erudite essay "The Magician from the Pear Garden" was made available in the VOKS informational pamphlet on Dr. Mei Lanfang's theater.

EISENSTEIN   Comrades! We are used to seeing progress—in art as well as in science and politics—as a linear advance. In reality, however, the progressive may well be moving sideways, backwards, or in a spiral. I would like to address myself to the ancient Chinese theater's paradoxical timeliness for our own art in our present stage of development.

The classical Chinese theater, sometimes erroneously called the Peking Opera, with Dr. Mei Lan-fang as its foremost representative and, at the same time, most severe reformer, is ruled by conventions that date back to the beginning of our Western era. Nevertheless, it affects a modern audience in demonstrably immediate and powerful ways. How can this paradox be explained? As materialists, we cannot rest content with stale theories about humanity's ahistorical and "perennial" nature.

What strikes one immediately, even in a first encounter with the Chinese theater, is the conventional and curiously "abstract" element in its mode of expression. A table, for example, may serve as a number of different things—it may be a dining table, or the bar in a courtroom, or an altar. Even more variable is the function of the *yingchen,* the horsehair broom. On one hand, it is an attribute of gods, demigods, and all kinds of spirit beings; on the other hand, the same broom may be used by a servant to indicate that she is sweeping the floor. But what is interesting about these examples is not only that one thing serves as a sign for another. More important is the *lability* or *mobility* of the meaning—the fact that the sign may stand for a whole slew of different things and concepts depending on which other signs surround it.

This phenomenon is not restricted to the theater; on the contrary, it has deep roots in Chinese culture. The foremost instance of this can of course be seen in the glyphs of Chinese writing, and in its "diffuse" words which receive their concrete meaning only after they have been combined with others. Thus the concepts of "fire," "bowl," "ship," and "down" are indicated by the same word, *zhuo.* The word *hao* may mean "good," "to love," "alms," "friendship," and "much." And so on.

Thus the multiplicity of meanings that is so striking in the Chinese theater's use of objects and stage props is intrinsic to Chinese expression. The word, the object, the sign do not combine into an exact and clearly delineated representation of concepts the way we are used to in our "occidental" type of logical thought. Instead, the sign—or the symbol formed by a couple of combined signs—has an immediate sensuous effect.

What, then, has this ancient way of thinking and creating impressions to teach us, as we are now constructing socialist realism, the most progressive art in human history? Well, an astonishingly large number of things.

The Chinese theater shows us that the demand for "verisimilitude," which haunts our art time and again, is not a symptom of an advanced understanding of art, but, on the contrary, of an undeveloped one. Vsyevolod Emilyevich has already spoken about this with sufficient emphasis.

VOICE FROM THE AUDIENCE   Yes, more than sufficient! [*Shushing and hubbub.*]

EISENSTEIN   [*Continues.*] The Chinese theater shows us an alternative to the narrowly rationalistic, reality-reproductive art developed in the Occident, which falls far short of the demands of the great socialist *Gesamtkunstwerk* we are now working on. In its severe traditionalism, the Chinese art leads us back to a level of *affective thinking,* to a unity of image, thought, and feeling as it has been preserved in the mobile and ambiguous Chinese signs. For an art that wants to affect and move today's masses forward, this language is infinitely superior to the linear, desiccated, and restrictive language of "verisimilitude." [*Hubbub and murmurs in the audience.*]

The Chinese theater guides us back to levels of our own thinking with which the creative artist must always remain in touch. It guides us back to the glittering golden caves of archaic consciousness, where we approach the secret of original unity, unity between image and expression, intellect and feeling, between the principles of *yin* and *yang,* between male and female. The ascent to spheres of higher consciousness, an ascent made on such different paths by Chinese and occidental art—one by remaining in touch with the sources, the other at the cost of a continuous longing for a new synthesis—is an ascent that we, as artists, have to undertake in the creation of every one of our works, our living images. The Chinese show us the way back to the necessary point of departure.

Finally, the Chinese theater shows us the way for the new synthetic art that *the art of film* has been destined to become by the very logic of history. The art of film, which combines all other art forms in itself, the film whose outlines we are as yet only guessing at—a film with three-dimensional color and sound—must, if it is to develop together with victorious socialism, absolutely obey the fundamental laws of emotional thinking. Fundamental laws which we can perceive in every single gesture made by the great Dr. Mei Lan-fang!

The synthetic art of all nations being developed today at our film schools and in our film studios has everything to learn from ancient Chinese culture's example, in the building of the great community of the future—Communist society! [*Scattered strong applause, hubbub.*]

NEMIROVICH-DANCHENKO   Sergei Mikhailovich's erudition equals the vertigo induced by his associational leaps. It is hard to fathom how verisimilitude in art can be seen as *primitive* compared to "the caves of archaic consciousness"! But perhaps some colleague with more experience in the fine points of dialectics will be able to explain this to us—or to correct Sergei Mikhailovich. I have already made a note of Comrade Kerzhentsev's name.

But before we get to that, we must hear from our specially invited guests from Western Europe.

When one says Gordon Craig, one thinks of modernism in the theater; when one says modernism in the theater, one thinks of Gordon Craig. For more than three decades the two have been practically synonymous. Ever since his production of Shakespeare's *Hamlet* at the Artistic Theater in 1912, Gordon Craig has been a legendary figure in the Russian theatrical world. We warmly welcome him back to Moscow! [*Applause.*]

CRAIG   Dear colleagues! I am grateful and proud to have been invited to Moscow, and particularly to this evening, Dr. Mei Lanfang meeting with his Russian admirers, whose ranks I beg to join.

To see Mei Lan-fang's theater is to step into a dream I never thought would come true: an instance of theater as "visual music," in which every detail is subordinated to the demands of the organic composition. Gentlemen, the magical effect of the mask cannot be denied! When Mei Lan-fang performs the White Lady, he leaves all "imitation," all stale psychology behind, and he becomes pure form. We witness the moment when, as Nietzsche put it, "Man is no longer an artist but becomes a work of art himself."

Quite understandably, this unique art comes to us from the East. Our own theater is haunted, every day and every hour, by the ghosts of literature and illustration. This applies, as I have noted during my stay here in Moscow, even to the Russian theater, one I greatly admire, one that more than any other in the Occident has become its own sovereign art form. May the heavenly discipline in Mei Lan-fang's art become an ideal to be striven toward, a lodestar for our actors.

Permit an old dreamer of the theater to bow to an artist who has made his dream a living reality! [*Bows. Strong applause.*]

MEYERHOLD   [*From his seat.*] Comrades! Let us remember these words from a stern master, who has returned, like Hamlet's father's ghost, to call us to arms against laziness, triviality, and routine! In the debate about the theater during this century, no concept may have been as misunderstood as Craig's "supermarionette." But we all know, or ought to know, that this concept is not directed *against* the actor but *to* him: it exhorts him to rise above himself, to master "this all-too weak flesh." That is what we would like to see in our actors, that is what Dr. Mei Lan-fang lets us experience every second! [*Applause.*]

TAIROV   [*From his seat.*] For once, I have to say—

NEMIROVICH-DANCHENKO   I must ask the colleague to respect the order of speakers.

TAIROV   —for once, I have to say that I am in *full agreement* with Comrade Meyerhold! [*Laughter, applause.*]

NEMIROVICH-DANCHENKO   Mr. Craig, as you can see, the memory of your visit almost twenty-five years ago lives on. Only a visiting performance like the one we have seen today could make a comparable impression on our theater workers. And not only on our own. We are privileged to have among us tonight two representatives of the German anti-Fascist theater movement. First, I call upon Erwin Piscator, the renowned theatrical director and author of the book *The Political Theater.*

PISCATOR   Comrades! In the anti-Fascist theater movement's consciousness, China has always inhabited an important place. Who in Berlin does not remember the Meyerhold Theater's visit in the spring of 1930 with Comrade Tretyakov's play *Roar, China!*—a performance that almost created a revolutionary situation in the auditorium! Friedrich Wolf's *Tai Yank Awakens* became, in our own production, an important weapon in the struggle against the tide of Fascism. At the World Theater Olympics in 1933 a young Chinese theater activist testified how his comrades had been dragged off the stage, assaulted, and shot or thrown into prison. It is a long way from China to Germany, but there were many among us who then felt that we had the same tale to tell.

On either side of history's first socialist state, the Soviet Union, our countries now wait for our marching orders, for the moment when the masses will take over the stage of history. In that situation, art, least of all the art of theater, cannot remain neutral.

From that point of view, how should we respond to Mei Lanfang's enchanting art?

I have become known as a spokesman for the political theater, for a theater that participates in the struggle of the moment. I have paid homage to Friedrich Wolf's thesis that art is a weapon. But my stay in the Soviet Union, my discussions with Soviet comrades, and my encounter with the full spectrum of Soviet theater—in which the Artistic Theater's realism peacefully coexists with Meyerhold's syntheticism and Okhlopkov's emotional political theater—has given me an opportunity to reflect upon the multiple task of art.

In a socialist society, where the revolution has already been victorious, one can not only afford to, but one is obliged to preserve and care for the accumulated experience of the past. [*Applause.*]

When, in 1927, I started the theater at Nollendorfplatz in Berlin, I wrote that "I perform political theater in order to liberate the theater from politics." There were many who criticized me for those words. But today the development of the Russian theater proves me right. Here one already feels a touch of eternity. Here it seems quite natural to speak about humanity's ideal of beauty. I believe that after the revolutionary transition phase, questions of life's beauty and perfection, of the harmony of form and content, will be uppermost in the program of Soviet art and theater.

But what does this have to do with Dr. Mei Lan-fang's art? His theater, after all, comes from China, where the socialist revolution is far from complete—I can hear some comrade say, who has been reading the Marxist manuals. Confronted by Mei Lan-fang's theater, I must admit that theory abandons me—or is it the Chinese theater that abandons theory?

Art is a weapon, but not only a weapon—it is also part of the goal for which we are fighting: justice, humanity, beauty. Let our art be a weapon in the fight for a society in which the beauty of Mei Lan-fang's great art becomes everybody's property, as Stanislavski's and Meyerhold's art has become in the Soviet Union! [*Warm applause.*]

NEMIROVICH-DANCHENKO We thank Comrade Piscator for his valuable comments. They testify to the anti-Fascist theater movement's rapid and sound development. I now call upon another prominent German man of the theater on the anti-Fascist front, a former collaborator of Piscator and the librettist of the well-known *Threepenny Opera,* Bertolt Brecht. [*Brecht walks up to the lectern, apparently with some reluctance.*]

BRECHT Several of the speakers have touched on the aspects of the Chinese theater that verge on magic and hypnosis. We have even heard this magical art recommended—due to its immediate effect on the subconscious by means of supposedly "archetypal" symbols—as a model for new theater and film. But there are obvious drawbacks to an art that transforms the audience into socialists while simultaneously causing them to lose consciousness. In our opinion, an art to be used against those hypnotists who now, literally or figuratively, hold large numbers of the European working class in thrall, should be aimed at *raising consciousness* rather than at *enchantment*. In the German proletarian theater we have, with among others our colleague Piscator, worked out certain techniques for such a consciousness-raising theater. For lack of a better term, we have called it the "epic" theater.

Now the question is whether we, given our particular premise, should content ourselves with admiring Dr. Mei Lan-fang's art as a survival from a past era—no longer useful, but beautiful in its traces of use—or if there is anything we can learn from it? In the Chinese theater's exterior trappings—the use of masks, gestural "abbreviations," scenery, etc.—there are certain devices the epic theater can use and has used. However, these could just as well be used by a theater with diametrically opposed intentions. I would prefer to say something about what the Chinese theater can teach us about a neglected area: the *art of being a spectator.*

The Chinese theater provides a viewer used to our occidental stage craft with a useful "purification" of the senses. In it, no effort is made to maintain the illusion that the performance is an actual event. The theater's technical aspect is shown without embarrassment—but not by "revealing" it in the equivocal and self-conscious manner that can be found on certain experimental stages in the West. In the Chinese theater, the audience becomes literally *visible to itself,* in a well-lit auditorium. This Chinese art does not depend on the naturalistic illusion to which the Western audience seems to be addicted as if it were opium—while it is quite prepared to do without it in similar situations, such as the circus, or the boxing arena.

It has been said that during his tour of the United States, Dr. Mei Lan-fang found himself obliged to explain that he was not a transvestite even though he performed female parts on the stage. Special press releases had to be issued to stress that Dr. Mei Lan-fang was in all respects a normal male, a good paterfamilias, and a banker by profession. We know that there still are places where it is necessary to prevent incidents by informing the public that the actor playing the villain is not himself a villain. This happens not only because some audiences are primitive but, in equal measure, because our Western art of acting is primitive. In the Chinese theater the spectator is freed from such compulsive reactions to direct his attention to other relationships.

Since there is no instigation to forget that the Chinese actor *is* an actor, one is free to observe how he translates everyday language into his own. When one sees him on stage, one actually sees no fewer than three persons simultaneously: one who shows and two who are being shown. Let me give you an example. We see, for instance, a girl preparing tea in the prescribed manner. She does this with certain ceremonial gestures, and these are perfect in themselves. Second, the actor shows us exactly in what way this girl is impatient, or calm, or in love. While doing so, he shows us, third, how an actor expresses impatience, calm, or infatuation by means of these prescribed gestures. On stage, the actor observes both the character's actions and his own acting.

In his introductory remarks, which I found very useful and enlightening, Comrade Tretyakov mentioned the theater's social impact in patterning everyday Chinese existence. We are, of course, interested in a different effect on the audience. But the Chinese theater can teach us to look at familiar conditions with astonishment: caused not only by the "mysteries" of the stage, which are in fact not veiled but revealed, but, first and foremost, by the social conditions that must be freed from their veils of "naturalness" and immutability.

On a previous visit to Moscow I had the opportunity to talk to Comrade Tretyakov and some of his friends among the literary critics. It became clear to me that Soviet scholars had developed a concept useful to the aesthetic of our time that must now replace the superannuated Aristotelian one. If you'll excuse my poor pronunciation, the Russian term for this concept is *ostranyenye.* In the new German theater we have provisionally used the term *Verfremdung,* "distancing," and simultaneously changed the content of the Soviet scholars' concept to some degree. Their primary interest seems to have been directed at the ability of art to provide a *feeling* of liberation by turning accustomed ways of seeing upside down, thus breaking the automatism of perception.

We are only interested in this sense of liberation, or astonishment, to the extent that it simultaneously enables the spectator to struggle against social oppression. This is where the Chinese theater's distancing methods seem extraordinarily useful. They teach us to see, in part, the astonishing elements in what we have been taught to see as natural, and in part, the difference between what is shown and who is showing it. In this astonishment, this perceptual gap, there is room for the assumption of a critical viewpoint—which is what bourgeois society and bourgeois theater fear, and for good reason.

This assumption of a critical viewpoint is not simply "given" to us by the appropriation of the distancing concept or of the Chinese theater's methods for achieving its effects. But anyone who has learned to think dialectically ought to agree that it is entirely possible to use a technique derived from the realm of magic to fight against magic, and to transform a concept of art as play into a concept of art that takes its promises seriously. [*Faint applause, with a few members of the audience applauding enthusiastically and for a long time.*]

NEMIROVICH-DANCHENKO   A brief response from Eisenstein. [EISENSTEIN *runs to the lectern on his short legs, speaks rapidly and with a shrill voice.*]

EISENSTEIN   Comrade Brecht has represented the Chinese actor's art, and my opinions of it, in a subjective and demagogical manner. Anyone who has witnessed Dr. Mei Lan-fang's performance and heard my comments must be aware of that.

Brecht's concern is the best imaginable—to find models for an *activating theater.* But in his well-meaning pursuit of this he wipes out the Chinese theater's essence, its symbolism, and transmutes into a soulless specimen. The creation of a "non-Aristotelian" theater is simply a *contradictio in adiecto,* as the ancient philosophers put it, a scholastic idea as absurd as the attempt to produce alcohol-free vodka! [*General laughter.*] Or, to pick an example perhaps a little closer to our German colleagues, to try to create a socialist revolution without a proletariat. It is not just that the loss is greater than the gain. The experiment can only be performed in the heads of isolated intellectuals, at the cost of the subject's soul—its *spiritus,* as it is indeed called in Latin! The desiccated specimens Comrade Brecht produces in his laboratory can never enthuse the masses.

As far as my attitude toward the "magical" element of theater and art goes, Brecht will have to admit that there are phenomena that cannot be captured within the conceptual behaviorist frame that attracted both him and me for a while. We discussed this matter thoroughly on a shared train journey a number of years ago, as I'm sure Brecht remembers.

Art is a language. We seem to be in agreement on that. But language does not consist only of words which can be exchanged and rearranged like building blocks. Language is also the treasure trove of collective memory—and this does not apply only to the Chinese I used as an example. Language contains meanings and relationships from which none of its speakers (and here I mean language in its widest sense, including even gestures and facial expressions) can ever detach himself. Why should he even want to try? Above all, why should we, we art workers, abstain from these powerful means of expression—I do not hesitate to call them "magical"—in favor of some intellectual *distancing?* Today we must mobilize all available means in the struggle for justice and progress! If Brecht can engage in that struggle with his means, I salute him. But it would be wrong to believe that he is following the Chinese theater's example in doing so. [*Applause.*]

BRECHT [*From his seat.*] As far as I remember, we mostly talked about Wagner on that train—a man of the theater whose magic really *has been* put to use in my homeland. If today I am able to develop my theatrical work only as thought experiments, this is very much due to the effective application of precisely that magic since we met three years ago.

My lasting impression of our conversation, back then, was that you suffered from what I called synthesis nostalgia. By that I meant that you longed to return to the cults at the sources of art, and those of theater in particular, even though the cult in your case was known as Proletkult. [*Laughter and applause.*] But when you say that the theater emerged from cult, all you are really saying is that it *became* theater exactly by leaving cult behind. Today it seems to me that you are projecting your synthesis nostalgia onto Dr. Mei Lan-fang's theater. For my own part, I am convinced that discrepancies, differences, and contraries—as opposed to that comprehensive synthesis—should provide the starting point for the art that won't only rouse the masses of today but will also teach them how to gain direction and power tomorrow. [*Scattered applause.*]

NEMIROVICH-DANCHENKO   I must ask the colleagues to adhere to the order of speakers! By his request, another *brief* response to Sergei Mikhailovich, from our other Sergei Mikhailovich—Tretyakov. Go ahead, please.

TRETYAKOV   This concerns the cult aspect. I strongly suspect that the Soviet audience has received a skewed impression of the Chinese theater, seeing it presented at a remove from its social context, in our "temples of art." In China the atmosphere of theatrical performances is anything but devotional. The performances often last for seven to eight hours. The air in the auditorium is incredibly hot and stale, and people walk in and out, snack on candy and fruit and drink tea during the play. Attendants toss hot damp washcloths to audience members who wish to wipe the sweat off their faces and bodies. Under these circumstances the attention paid to the play does not resemble our engrossed "empathy." It alternates between total concentration and inattention, as it does at the boxing arenas Comrade Brecht mentioned. Between the "rounds" of theatrically meaningful events, people have lively discussions about the heroes' actions and, not least, the various actors' performances.

NEMIROVICH-DANCHENKO   We thank you for this information, which may serve to emphasize how difficult it is to draw any immediate parallels between the two great artforms that are tonight's subjects—the Chinese theater, and the evolving socialist-realist theater.

Before Comrade Kerzhentsev from the Committee for Artistic Matters gives us his closing remarks, we call upon yet another representative of the international theater movement, the young Swedish stage director Alf Sjöberg. [SJÖBERG *ascends to the lectern.*]

SJÖBERG   For a young man of the theater from the austere North, these few days here in Moscow have provided experiences that will leave their mark on a lifetime.

It is often said that our great August Strindberg is only the exception to prove the rule that our Swedish theater is utterly provincial. But I firmly believe that today no one, not even in Sweden, has any doubts that the future belongs to an *international* theater. The theater lives by the meeting of opposites, by the encounter between the old and the new, between East and West. To watch, one evening, Gordon Craig's company with Michoels's stirring King Lear, and then, the next night, to witness the genius of Mei Lan-fang—this could only happen in the Moscow of 1935!

The freedom with which the Chinese theater deals with time and space reminds one both of the flying carpets of fairy tales and of the hectic pulse and dizzying ambivalence of the modern metropolis. I am in complete agreement with Eisenstein's view that film has much to learn from this Chinese art—ancient and exultantly youthful, closed and global at the same time. The art of film, one that seems predestined to express the new zeitgeist, will only evolve by staying in touch with the deep sources of the theater.

Every country's theater has its own undercurrents, even where a narrow bourgeois conception of art has lost touch with them. We, the young Swedish theater people, who fight for the idea of a people's theater and want to be part of the international theater movement, must work with our heritage in the same way today's young Chinese theater workers make use of their own, whose steward is the great magician—Dr. Mei Lan-fang! [*Applause.*]

NEMIROVICH-DANCHENKO   We thank you for your testimonial to the anti-Fascist theater movement in a country about which we still don't know enough despite its geographical proximity. I now call upon Comrade Platon Mikhailovich Kerzhentsev, who during his foreign service years did get to know Sweden by living there. [*Brief applause.*] At this time, however, he will speak in his capacity of vice chairman of the State Committee for Artistic Affairs.

KERZHENTSEV   Dear Dr. Mei Lan-fang! Comrade Chairman! Comrades, theater workers!

If nothing else, tonight's lively discussion has shown the depth of the impression Dr. Mei Lan-fang's unforgettable visit has made on the world of Soviet theater and even on the representatives of Europe's anti-Fascist theater movement we are honored to have as our guests. The Chinese visit has been a historic event, and—as Comrade Nemirovich-Danchenko already pointed out in his introductory remarks—one that may be said to symbolize today's and tomorrow's avowal of friendship between the Soviet and the Chinese peoples.

We, the Soviet people, led by the Communist Party and its hard-as-steel leader, Comrade Stalin, promise our Chinese friends that we will do everything in our power to strengthen these links! [*Strong, rhythmic applause.*]

Vladimir Illich [*laughter; applause and laughter in the audience*]—I mean, Vladimir Ivanovich also pointed out, quite correctly, that the Soviet theater, and with it, the whole world's progressive theater, faces a task involving great responsibility: that of creating great socialist-realist drama! Today every rehearsal, every discussion among our theater workers must be directed toward this goal. And in every sector of the front in the struggle against fascism, the principles of humanism and realism must be defended against all kinds of fragmenting influences, sabotage, and pseudoradical deviations. From this point of view, tonight's discussion has not been entirely satisfactory.

Comrade Meyerhold is among those who have most clearly declared themselves in agreement with the principles of socialist realism. However, his *practice* does not speak the same unequivocal language. The Soviet public is calling for practical actions. Only two years from now we will celebrate the great October Revolution's twentieth anniversary, and the Party expects that on every Soviet stage, every Soviet theater worker will do his very best to present, at that time, the great socialist-realist anniversary drama. A failure to do so, or a lack of enthusiasm for this great task, will not be interpreted as anything but an expression of contempt for the masses, and as a violation of political unity.

One particular exchange of ideas has been particularly notable tonight. There is, of course, some truth in Comrade Piscator's remark that we in the Soviet Union, having completed our revolution, wish to preserve what is valuable in our past, while in countries such as Germany the struggle against the oppressors and their "culture" has taken center stage. But in the face of the Fascist threat, all progressive forces must stand united. Personally, I do not believe that they can do so within the framework of Comrade Brecht's "non-Aristotelian" theater *or* the one provided by Comrade Eisenstein's ideas, which I am tempted to call "Platonic"—at the risk of ridicule occasioned by my own old-fashioned first name. [*Laughter.*]

Eisenstein is a magnificent creator of films. His chronicle of the revolution, *Battleship Potemkin,* is one of the Soviet film archive's treasures. Presently he is an esteemed teacher—but despite his legendary erudition, as a theoretician of art he lacks certain elementary Marxist insights. Should the great socialist-realist drama of the future draw its nourishment from the caves of the subconscious, from which humanity has ascended to such heights as the October Revolution—which, in itself, is but *one* step toward even greater heights?? *No, and again, no!* Our Party and its press have unequivocally, and a long time ago, distanced themselves from Freudian and similar notions about the subconscious, notions that now only serve to nourish the decadent atmosphere of the Fascist camp.

Comrade Brecht is quite right in rejecting such talk about the collective subconscious, and in taking the side of reason. But who, in our time, represents reason in its highest form? Surely not petit-bourgeois intellectuals, even though they may have mastered the laws of dialectics and now, in their own fashion, have a desire to join the working masses. The danger lies in their desire to do it *their* way, not in the way the progress of history itself dictates: by following the leadership of the Communist Party. [*Applause.*]

Comrade Brecht's analysis of how the Chinese theater works is certainly interesting and subtle, but when he wants to install his formalist theory as a lodestar for anti-Fascist theater, we must voice an objection. His fetishization of artistic technique at the expense of art's ideological task, and, above all, art's obligation to mirror reality, strikes us Soviet cultural workers as both familiar and ominous. It is no accident that Comrade Brecht finds he has so much in common with Comrade Tretyakov, whose contribution tonight, despite its overload of facts, still reflected a lingering influence of futurist and Proletkult ideas. I can say this with even greater conviction since I myself was once afflicted by the Bogdanovian contagion and tried to spread it within the young Soviet theater. Thanks to the Party's Leninist and Stalinist criticism I did, however, regain my health. Thus I would like to express my best wishes for lasting good health to Comrade Tretyakov, who performs important tasks on the anti-Fascist cultural front.

Dear Dr. Mei Lan-fang! To some extent, tonight's discussion has been a discussion *pro domo suo,* to employ a language of which Soviet theater workers—as you may have noticed—are quite fond. [*Laughter.*] However, I do not hesitate to say that it is precisely thanks to your masterful art that we can now demand more of our Soviet theater than ever before. What the Soviet public is waiting for is a theater with your artistic perfection and militant humanistic content, in short, a socialist-realist theater! [*Prolonged, rhythmic applause.*]

NEMIROVICH-DANCHENKO   And therewith I declare our discussion closed. But I would like to leave the very last word to the incomparable Dr. Mei Lan-fang, our guest of honor, without whom this meeting could not have taken place. A big hand for Dr. Mei Lan-fang! [*Rhythmic applause. Long pause.*] May I ask Dr. Mei Lan-fang to come up to the lectern? [*Pause. Hubbub. A functionary hurries up to the podium and whispers something in* NEMIROVICH-DANCHENKO'*s ear. The latter clears his throat. Brief silence.*] I regret to have to inform you that Dr. Mei Lan-fang was obliged to leave the auditorium so as not to miss the night train to Peking with his ensemble. May I suggest to Comrade Arosev that we send a warm telegram of congratulation and thanks to our guest, from all of us at this meeting, which I now declare closed! [*Applause.*]

Ash Wednesday

Thousands of stars glitter on the vaulted planetarium ceiling. Rows of seats in a half-circle. In the middle of the open space stands a Zeiss projector—a large, shiny black piece of equipment reminiscent of a robot or a space capsule, mounted on a tall stand.

EISENSTEIN *sits in the first row, half-asleep, or else engrossed in reading a large notebook with oilcloth covers. He is wearing a bright blue, capelike overcoat. A slouch hat rests on the seat next to him.*

The silence is broken by distant music: "The Ride of the Valkyries," from Richard Wagner's Valkyrie. *As the music grows louder and more energetic,* EISENSTEIN *starts marking the rhythm with his left hand. He sets the book aside and follows the music with both hands, then gets up and starts "conducting" with expansive gestures.*

BAKHTIN *enters from the left, unnoticed. He is wearing a large, threadbare jacket. He is limping and leaning on a cane. He stops in front of* EISENSTEIN, *though not directly in front of him, and studies him and the room. After a while* EISENSTEIN *notices the visitor. His arms fall to his sides, the music fades away.*

EISENSTEIN   Who are you?

BAKHTIN   You invited me to come here.

EISENSTEIN   Oh. It's you, is it? But—weren't you supposed to come tomorrow?

BAKHTIN   Today is Tuesday.

EISENSTEIN   Really? [*Pause. Points at the cane:*] I didn't know that—I could have sent a car.

BAKHTIN   Don't worry, it's an old injury. What an interesting space this is. [*Pause.*] A temple for the age of science.

EISENSTEIN   The planetarium has a long history. It was, of course, a Renaissance invention, from the time before the separation of astronomy and astrology. But these great electric projectors only came along after the First World War. Precision optics by a Dr. Bauersfeld, employed by the firm of Carl Zeiss. *Das deutsche Wunder.* [*Chuckles.*]

BAKHTIN   If man can't reach the stars, the stars have to come down to him.

EISENSTEIN   It's really a kind of time machine. Here you can recreate the night sky at any time and place in history. Paris on the fourteenth of July 1789; the endless sky above Austerlitz that Andrei Bolkonsky contemplated; the Star of Bethlehem—whatever you want: Dr. Bauersfeld's machine takes you there in a moment! I enjoy coming here sometimes, when the—considerably dimmer—stars of Mosfilm have worn me out. I have the planetarium director's permission to come here after closing time. During regular hours there are always hordes of schoolchildren on field trips, attending lectures—"Pioneers of the New Age: Copernicus, Galileo, Newton," or "Lomonossov, Father of Russian Astronomy."

BAKHTIN   I just noticed the poster for tomorrow's subject: "Did Christ Exist?" [*Pause. Looks up at the vaulted ceiling.*] What is it we're seeing here?

EISENSTEIN   The constellations above the town of Nola at the time of Giordano Bruno's birth, anno Domini 1548. His horoscope is hard to interpret. Do you know about the stars?

BAKHTIN   Nothing new under the sun.

EISENSTEIN   That, like most famous statements, is actually wrong! It is true that Giordano's farewell letter to his students in Wittenberg ends with those words. But he himself only wrote, "What shall be? What has been. What has been? What shall be." When Lorenzo di Pupo, his assistant, made a fair copy of the letter, he added, "*Nihil sub sole novum.*" This was before Giordano went back to Italy. And was betrayed.

BAKHTIN   But the quote is older than that. Nothing new under the sun. [*They look up at the ceiling. Long pause.*] We have read your manuscript. [EISENSTEIN *gives a start, goes pale.* BAKHTIN *smiles.*]

Well, I hope you don't mind that I let my wife, Yelena Alek-sandrovna, read it, too. She worshiped Wagner when she was young, and saw the *Ring* several times—so she was able to refresh my memory. In recent years performances of Wagner have been few and far between, at least in our part of the world. [*Pause.*] So you want to stage the *Valkyrie* at the Bolshoi Theater. *Das lässt tief blicken,* as the Germans say. But if you want to know my opinion on your staging ideas, I'm afraid I have to disappoint you. I don't know anything about the theater.

EISENSTEIN   Never mind. Have a seat anyway. Let me show you what our cosmic theater can do.

[*They sit down.*]

BAKHTIN   So this is where you're preparing your Wagner? [*Pause.*] Do you know what this place reminds me of? Those gigantic mausoleums for which they drew up plans after the French Revolution, dedicated to the Supreme Being. Wagner, too, may well belong in a mausoleum. But who knows—perhaps he, too, is awaiting his joyful resurrection.

EISENSTEIN   [*With enthusiasm.*] With the *Valkyrie* that is abso-lutely the case! It is a work that deals with the threshold between the old and the new—after Wotan is no longer able to rule, but Siegfried hasn't been born yet. As you see, our plan is based on the premise that the *Ring* is really about the curse of private property—an interpretation that strikes me as pretty unassailable.

BAKHTIN   Yes, probably even to the German ambassador.

EISENSTEIN   You said it. That is why it must be expressed with precision. In the *Valkyrie* two principles are at war: love and order. On one hand we have the twins, Siegmund and Sieglinde, and their forbidden love, on the other, Fricka with her family values. Wotan's capitulation, and Brünhilde's, the valkyrie's, sacrifice are, one might say, male and female methods for the resolution of an insoluble conflict. In Marxist terms one might say that the sib-lings represent an anarchic mode of production which is doomed to extinction, while Fricka represents a formalist-bourgeois one, and Brünhilde stands for the humanist-communist mode of the future! The German ambassador may not like that view very much. I suppose we'll have to provide him with his own set of program notes for the gala opening.

BAKHTIN   That's the remarkable thing about Wagner. His work seems capable of accommodating any number of interpretations, one inside the other, like a set of Chinese boxes.

EISENSTEIN   Precisely. Psychoanalysts, for instance, would say that the siblings' love represents the id, Fricka the superego, and Wotan and Brünhilde two aspects of the ego. And a historian of religion would recognize this as the evolution from polytheism to atheism. And so on.

BAKHTIN   The only requirement being that all interpretations refer the drama back to itself.

EISENSTEIN   But, no—how so? On the contrary, what we are doing is opening up Wagner—in depth! Back to mythical thinking itself! In the archetypal images of the world tree, the wheel, the hermaphroditic bodies of the siblings, in this as yet unbroken connection between color, form, and imagination we can chart the fundamental principles of all art. In order to get a grip on the Soviet viewer's consciousness we must manage to get his nervous system to vibrate in unison with Wagner's music, thus leading it out onto this boundless ocean. The past will reach out to the present, and on to the future, to the artworks of the future—over the heads of the nineteenth century! Only then can the myth become flesh, only then can we realize our old dream of the theater as action!

BAKHTIN   But isn't Wagner's ocean, by its very nature, very nineteenth-century? It's a big ocean, but a theatrical one—like the ones in the great circus arenas of London and Paris, where they had real live racehorses on moving runways, but also real naval battles performed in gigantic pools. *That* is the kind of ocean Wagner has in mind, or so it seems to me. Wouldn't that be something to show at the Bolshoi, now that the ice has been broken, so to speak?

EISENSTEIN   But it's a question of liberating Wagner from all those wrappings—to strip the nineteenth-century costume off the myth!

BAKHTIN   Are you sure the myth is ready to perform in its birthday suit? Instead of trying to give the myth some kind of *Ur*-form, one should perhaps try to present the image of Wagner's myth—or more precisely, the image of Wagner's image of the myth. It may just be possible to revive the myth within such a live relationship. To show it as it once *did* live—as image, as word, as sign. Myth is already the *word* about the action, not the action itself.

EISENSTEIN   You were right. You really don't understand the theater at all.

BAKHTIN   No, I don't. [*Pause.*] But your project is worth considering. You say that the past will reach out to the present—the circle will close, history will bite its own tail. The Eternal Return—is that it? Well, we may have reached that stage. Just before the turning point. In which case the *Valkyrie* becomes a kind of cult play, with yourself as the high priest. But tell me, *whose* high priest are you? [EISENSTEIN *is silent.*] Come to think of it, this room might be a better performance space for it than the Bolshoi.

EISENSTEIN   The planetarium? Yes, that has occurred to me. But where would we put the orchestra? You're forgetting the music. *La musique avant toute chose!*

BAKHTIN   I may not have an ear for music—

EISENSTEIN   It is the music that nourishes the tragedy. Wagner demands a large format. Reversing Goethe's comment, one might say that Wagner's music is "architecture in motion." It needs to be made visible, its visual character demands contours, colors, volume. [*Shouts into the echoing space:*] Volume!!! [*Pause.*]

BAKHTIN   I may not have an ear for music, but I must have enough of one not to appreciate Wagner. Despite his endless melodies, his flowing harmonies, his chromatic glissandi, he is, after all, horrendously static. Just between you and me, I have never managed to sit all the way through one of those endless performances. Life is so short, after all. *Ars longa, vita brevis*—

EISENSTEIN   —as another Wagner said, that poor student of Doctor Faustus's. Which reminds me of what I really wanted to ask you. Our pact with Germany has at least made it permissible to openly discuss the greatness of German culture. On the other hand, my last film, *Alexander Nevski,* has been put in cold storage as a consequence of that pact. My film's representation of the atrocities committed by the Teutonic Knights has become a little . . . untimely. Well, it may get another chance. [*Chuckles.*]

BAKHTIN   It is just a matter of being able to wait.

EISENSTEIN   What's important right now, in any case, is that I can finally stage Wagner. And that you can publish your book on Goethe. I heard it mentioned by a good friend at the publishing house. For me, Goethe and Wagner are German culture's greatest contributions to humanity. Two polymath geniuses, both of whom dedicated their lives to basically the same fundamental problem: unity in multiplicity. In art, in poetry, in music, in the creative method in general.

BAKHTIN   Goethe and Wagner? I can't deny that they can be seen in such a context—today. But in the greater context of time, the time of culture, they do not meet.

EISENSTEIN   But there are obvious connections: take the idea of the *Gesamtkunstwerk*—

BAKHTIN   In Goethe? Only in the late romantics' attempt to *finish* Goethe. A total misunderstanding! To be honest with you, Wagner and Goethe can only be considered as opposites. They are the two sides of the German spirit: enlightened clarity versus cloudy brooding, polyphonic Europeanism against dark nationalism. Germany as spirituality, and Germany as passion. [*Pause.*] Goethe is the eye; Wagner, the ear. Nietzsche would have called them the dream and the drunkenness, Apollo and Dionysus. [*In a low voice:*] One hopes that the Germany we see triumphing today is only an accidental crossbreed, not a synthesis—it is a drunken dream. [*Pause.*]

Just look at the difference in Goethe's and Wagner's attitudes toward myth—this should be of great importance to your enterprise. Goethe does not genuflect to myth. He knows it, down to the tiniest detail, and treats it with affectionate irony. Take, for instance, the witches' sabbath in *Faust,* part 2: it is more of a parody than high seriousness. When Wagner, on the other hand, finds myth, he finds himself. The language of myth is his mother tongue, he does not know any other language, but he turns this into a strength. When Wagner says *einmal,* this does not refer to the fairy tale's "once upon a time," but to that of the myth: once it was thus—and to it, all will return.

Wagner is Wagner. But Goethe is Mozart. Do you remember what he told Eckermann, that the only one able to compose a Faust opera would have been Mozart? For Mozart, everything is critical, everything is in motion. With him, every human being is a bundle of contradictions. In some ways Mozart prefigures the nineteenth-century novel: Goethe, Balzac, even Dostoevsky. I'm not saying that Wagner only points to the past. He points to the future, but in another way. He points to the mirror, not to his fellow man—if you see what I mean.

EISENSTEIN   I still think you should have sat through one of those Wagner performances. You don't seem to recognize his polyphony. His music is a boundless forest of voices, leitmotifs, returns, reminiscences—a boundless forest! And that prefigures not only the modern novel, Joyce above all, but the *Gesamtkunstwerk* of our time—the film, of course, and its central problem, which is vertical montage.

BAKHTIN   A forest? Yes, but a forest with no trail leading out of it, a forest in which everything refers back to the subject itself. Someone once said that Wagner's music does not dance. That isn't quite true. It does dance, but only in front of itself, in front of the mirror, in a dance that does not die and does not give new life. Everything points forward or back, but in some kind of curved space. [*Looks up at the vaulted ceiling.*] It is, if you'll permit me the jest, a spherical music. Implacably, everything returns to its point of origin, time and time again.

EISENSTEIN   You are looking for my *image* of Wagner, an image of his image of myth, perhaps even with a touch of parody. Remember that what I sent you is only an outline—besides, one composed for the Council on Repertory. As soon as the Bolshoi's artists take over, we won't have to wait very long for farcical effects! It is incredible how knock-kneed these people are, people who can sing like gods. Yesterday I had to rehearse Brünhilde forever to get her to do the simplest thing in the world. [*Gets up to demonstrate the scenery and the singer's motions, grotesquely.*] As you have seen, Yggdrasil, the world tree, stands center stage. Brünhilde, singing all the while, has to take a drinking horn from the tree, then hold it between her legs with the opening pointing down at an angle, and with a swaying motion of her body invite the exhausted Siegmund to refresh himself after the battle. The symbolism is pretty obvious, no? This woman insisted on making the same mistakes over and over again, while also stamping her foot to show that I had miscounted a few beats. The real problem was simply that she didn't want to spread her legs properly. [*Suddenly hysterical.*] I'll show those bitches how to spread their legs so wide they won't be able to get up again! And the bass singers, too! And the audience! Oh, you'll see. I'll take them on a trip they'll never forget. I'll hoist this fucking Wagner on his own petard, I'll dig down deeper than anyone has ever been, even in his wildest nightmares. A drunken dream, you said? Here you'll see a drunken nightmare pulling the wagon! When I short-circuit the flow between sun and moon, straight through the hearts of the copulating siblings, there won't be a whole lot left of the Bolshoi Theater! But the power of art will have been demonstrated! [*Slumps back into his seat.*]

BAKHTIN [*After a long pause*]. So, it's back to the beginning of everything? That sounds modern to a disconcerting degree. But do you think it'll be possible to do?

EISENSTEIN What does one not do to realize an old boyhood dream? [*Pause.*] Not too long ago I came across an old article on the *Valkyrie* by Vyacheslav Ivanov, written in 1919. I remember how I read it, back then, with tears in my eyes, during the Civil War, on tour with Proletkult's front-line theater. You see, old Ivanov didn't think that Wagner had gone all the way. He thought Wagner was only a forerunner of Ivanov's dream, the feast of the great collective Dionysiac body. [*Pulls a yellowed newspaper cutting out of his pocket.*] Listen to this: "In the wordless chorus of instruments—as is the composer's intention—humanity's collective will can already be heard. Melting into the symphony's soul, we can see the new man, as if our own ideal image were reflected into the world of the beyond. . . . Siegmund must die, but Sieglinde is saved to give life to Siegfried. The Sun Hero dies, just as the Sun itself dies, and drags all of Valhalla with him into destruction; but on Valhalla's ruins, a new race—" [*Pause.*] Hard to read here.

BAKHTIN   [*From memory*]. "—a new race will grow. A great prophecy. And yet, we are not waiting for such festivals. We are not waiting for the play of promise, but for the play of fulfillment, a play for and by the million-headed chorus, the voice of human, living polyphony. We are waiting—and I am certain that we are not waiting in vain." [*Long pause.*] Yes, a great prophecy, a great utopia. But old Vyacheslav didn't really have an ear for the voice from the million-headed chorus, its lament and triumphal shouts and laughter. Prophecies never come true the way prophets imagine. [*Pause.*] Now I remember where I have seen you before. In Vitebsk, in 1920. You were the director of a front-line theater that performed Mayakovsky, right? And after the show, during a debate with the audience, you read them that very passage!

EISENSTEIN   What a coincidence. [BAKHTIN *is silent.*] Vitebsk, January 1920—wait. [*Gets up, walks over to the projector's control panel. Opens a large catalog, turns its pages. Turns wheels, pushes a few switches. Looks up at the ceiling. The projector starts turning, the sky changes. Pause.*] Vitebsk, January 1920. You must have known that strange fellow Zubakin—archeologist, divinator, and Rosicrucian? He initiated me into a few things. [*Chuckles.* BAKHTIN *gives* EISENSTEIN *a skeptical look.*] Yes. Boris Zubakin. May he rest in peace. He used to tell me about your literary circle whose goal it was to rewrite all of Russian literary history according to astrological principles. Isn't that right? To put an end to all those meaningless movements and isms—classicism, romanticism, realism. To restructure it all according to truly scientific criteria! Rams, bulls, lions, and scorpions! I still remember the triad of signs that guides Russian literature: Pushkin, Chadayev, Belinski—Gemini. Lermontov, Tsvetaeva, Pilnyak—Libras. Zhukovski, Chekhov, Ivanov, Pasternak—Aquarians, one and all. And then, of course, the largest group of all, those dangerous Scorpios: Avakum the Protopope, Lomonosov, Dostoevsky, Andrei Biely, Khlebnikov. What more could you wish for? [BAKHTIN *contemplates the ceiling.*] And wasn't it the case that only Scorpios were allowed to attend the meetings of that circle? Otherwise Zubakin would have taken me along. [*Pause. Sits down.*] Tell me, what finally became of that project?

BAKHTIN   "The Society for Gay Literary Science," we called ourselves. No, those days will never return. [*Pause. Looks at* EISENSTEIN.] Sometimes the world is pretty small.

EISENSTEIN   There are no coincidences. Everything is destiny.

BAKHTIN   So you believe that there is a meaning inscribed up there, just waiting to be deciphered? [*Points at the ceiling.*] No. Not in the stars. Not in you. Not in me. What meaning there is, is created between us, between things and us. [*Pause. Takes a stone out of his pocket.*] Look at this stone. What do you see?

EISENSTEIN   An oval stone. Dark brown.

BAKHTIN   Feel it. [EISENSTEIN *hesitates.*] Come on, feel it. [EISENSTEIN *reluctantly takes the stone, holds it in his hand.*] What do you feel?

EISENSTEIN   It is heavy. Smooth. Pleasant to hold.

BAKHTIN   What meaning inheres in this stone? None at all—for you. Your description of it is objectively correct. But for me it is another stone. It was given to me by a woman who had found it on the Black Sea shore. I have carried it with me ever since, a rather long way, a rather long time. It has acquired meaning by becoming part of the context of my life. When she picked it up there by the Black Sea, she gave it a meaning. When she gave it to me, it acquired yet another meaning, and when I received it, it acquired yet another one.

EISENSTEIN   [*Turns the stone in his hand.*] Maybe it is the Wise Men's Stone? [*Chuckles.*] But didn't you know it is bad luck to walk around with a stone in your pocket?

BAKHTIN   There, you see? You are also giving it a meaning. [*Holds out his hand.* EISENSTEIN *reluctantly returns the stone.*] Are you saying that a meaning inheres in that stone regardless of its relationship to me, to you, to the human world? You may be right. But if so, how can we comprehend that meaning? Where is the center from which the meaning would emerge? And if it exists, do you believe that it is given to us humans to assume that position? We have to be content with what is relative, with approximations, with questions and answers. Meaning arises between questions and answers, in a dialogue.

EISENSTEIN   No, there is no center. Giordano Bruno already knew that. But there are structures!

BAKHTIN   There are?

EISENSTEIN   Well—only the gods know. [BAKHTIN *coughs.*] But context, approximations, dialogue—that's just *Einfühlung.* German idealism!

BAKHTIN   No, it is not only that. You may be right in saying that there are structures—in the world of natural science. Let me give you an easy example. You say, "Life is beautiful," and I say, "Life is beautiful." There is, indeed, a structure to that—linguists can describe it. The dictionary tells us what the words mean in an objective sense. But none of us speaks in an objective sense. Nevertheless, the venerable grammarians, as Giordano used to call them, persist in seeing words as something like chess pieces or coins that circulate in society, always equal to themselves. But the words we utter aren't coins. They are more like a kind of gift that wanders from hand to hand in an endless chain. And *that* is how words acquire their value—not by stock market listings. That is how this stone has received its value. Meaning is created not by words but by their utterance, not by motion but by action. All the words we utter, all the gestures we make, have been used before us, or by ourselves in other contexts. When you say "Life is beautiful"—

EISENSTEIN   You want me to say "Life is beautiful"?

BAKHTIN   You just said it. I can reply to you, agree with your irony, or reject it. Even if both you and I should say, "Life is beautiful," in all seriousness, those utterances would still remain two entirely different ones, because we are two different persons. One might imagine a state of complete understanding, but that would be based not on the identities of those words but on your complete understanding of me, and mine, of you. Ultimately, meaning nevertheless rests in you-for-me and me-for-you, not in me, not in you, and not in the words, either. Or in this stone.

[*Pause.*] Forgive me, I've been uttering too many words. Martin Buber said it better: "In the beginning is relation." [*Long pause during which both contemplate the artificial starry sky.*]

EISENSTEIN [*To himself.*] Words, words, words. Or was it: worlds, worlds, worlds?

BAKHTIN Do you know what day it is tomorrow? Ash Wednesday. It just occurred to me. Yes, the day Giordano was burned at the stake. [*Pause.*] May I suggest a little refreshment before penance and fasting begins? A modest repast for Fat Tuesday, by courtesy of a honorarium I just received. [*Produces, a little like a magician, a parcel that looks too big to have come out of his coat pocket; then, in the same manner, a flask from an inside pocket. Unwraps the parcel and takes out a large, dark sausage of dubious appearance—an andouillette, a French sausage made of animal entrails—and a chunk of bread. Puts the items on a chair, reverently cuts the sausage and the bread with a penknife. Pulls a cheap candle out of his pocket, lights it, and places it on the chair. Regards his handiwork with satisfaction.*]

EISENSTEIN Oh, so you're a magician as well! *Bravo dottore!* [*Claps his hands.*] A proper *cena de ceneri.*

BAKHTIN We should have some wine, too, but this Georgian brandy will have to do. [*Hands* EISENSTEIN *a piece of bread with some sausage on it, unscrews the top of his flask and offers it to* EISENSTEIN, *who takes a symbolic hit.* BAKHTIN *drinks a little more deeply. They eat.*]

EISENSTEIN Aaah. A genuine andouillette! Where the hell were you able to find it?

BAKHTIN [*Coughs briefly.*] We have our connections.

EISENSTEIN You can say that again. [*Pause.*] This includes everything. Both the taste of the intestines and the taste of what has passed through them. One can't really be sure whether one is eating or being eaten. [*Laughs shrilly.*] I'm sure you remember the scene of Gargantua's birth? The Fat Tuesday feast where everybody eats themselves sick, on credit. Sausages, intestines, shit, and birth pangs, all in a blissful stew. Just thinking about it makes one feel sated.

BAKHTIN [*Laughs, hands the flask to* EISENSTEIN.] That scene really is a summary of all of Rabelais, of his whole carnivalesque worldview. The literal meaning of *carnival* is "farewell to flesh." It is usually interpreted as farewell to flesh—meat—before the beginning of fast and penance. Fat Tuesday followed by Ash Wednesday. But, as Rabelais demonstrates, the deeper meaning is that if we wish to be reborn, we must bid farewell to *our own* flesh. To die, and to become again. In the borderline situation of the carnival, birth and death, eating stomachs and eaten stomachs, mingle in a one great long dance without beginning or end. Here, none come first or last, there is no beginning and no conclusion. The world is open, everything rests in the womb of the future, and everything will forever remain there. That is the message of the people's carnival.

EISENSTEIN   And it is so amazingly constant in all cultures: France, Russia, Mexico, Germany. A global genetic code.

BAKHTIN   If there was anything Wagner did not understand, it was precisely that. [*Takes a piece of sausage and chews it with a thoughtful mien.*] Goethe, on the other hand, *he* knew what it was about. Throughout his life he retained his feeling for the popular festival's objective symbolism. I'm not just thinking of his *Italian Journey,* or *Wilhelm Meister*—the theater world as a miniature carnival. Even in his most sublime poems you can hear the carnival's dual message. [*Recites:*]

Und so lang du das nicht hast,
Dieses stirb und werde,
Bist du nur ein trüber Gast
Auf der dunklen Erde.

[And as long as you do not have that, / This "die and become," / You are merely a sad guest / On this dark earth.]

EISENSTEIN   "Bist du nur ein trüber Gast auf der dunklen Erde!" [*Strikes the side of the flask with the blade of the penknife.*] Your health! oStirb und werde! [*Drinks. Hands the flask to* BAKHTIN. *Gets up, pulls his slouch hat down low over his eyes, raises the sleeve of his coat in front of his face like a masked Venetian reveler, and performs an elegant little mime that ends with an attempt to blow out the candle. Shouts shrilly:*] "Sia ammazzatto, dottore!" [BAKHTIN *retains his composure, shields the candle flame. Both laugh.*]

BAKHTIN   Cheers! Although I am no *dottore*. [*Drinks. Pause.*] Is it all right to smoke here? [*Takes a tobacco pouch and a couple of thin pieces of paper out of his pocket, flattens one of them, and rolls himself a cigarette.*]

EISENSTEIN   [*Ogles the other piece of paper, picks it up, reads:*] "Goethe's *werden* as the highest expression . . . the never to be completed striving . . . Faustianism first transcended by Dostoevsky." Was this a book?

BAKHTIN   What can you do? There's a paper shortage. [*Lights his cigarette on the candle, exhales a large puff of smoke.*] Manuscripts don't burn, they say, but this one works just fine. [*Pause.*] I'm sure we all have our German to wrestle with. I never thought it would turn into a whole book about Goethe, but there are times when the text determines its own direction. [*Pause.*] This is just a copy. The original rests with your friends at the state publishing house. I received the honorarium today. But they won't publish it.

EISENSTEIN   Why not? In the present situation a book on Goethe should be as acceptable as a performance of Wagner.

BAKHTIN   While they were reading my manuscript, the head of the house had already managed to commission another one from Comrade Lukács. I'm sure he'll manage to write a book that meets today's demands much better. In that sense, he has perfect pitch. Besides, I was never completely satisfied with mine, either. To write literary history has become so difficult, desperately difficult. Not to get it printed—I can wait. But the basic questions themselves are falsely posed. This endless discussion around realism—it is pure scholasticism. The same goes for Comrade Lukács's evolutionary scheme, in which the novel is supposed to follow the motion of the world's spirit—rise, maturity, decay, at ever higher elevations. Not that our Vitebsk project got us anywhere, either. [*Laughs. Pause.*] Tell me, why don't you put on Goethe's *Faust* instead? There we might arrive at a dialogue. But Wagner—

EISENSTEIN   No. Once you have the devil in your boat, you have to row him ashore. To tell you the truth, I can't quite figure out this *Valkyrie* myself. There is one part in it I can't get a grip on. "The Ride of the Valkyries." May I play it for you? I brought it with me. [BAKHTIN *nods.* EISENSTEIN *pulls a portable gramophone from under the seat, opens it, winds it up, sets down the needle. The gramophone starts playing the opening bars of Billie Holiday's "All of Me." He suddenly stops the record.*] I'm sorry, I must have made a mistake.

BAKHTIN   But what was that?

EISENSTEIN   Oh, it's just a jazz recording someone sent me from the States. Sorry—

BAKHTIN   [*Interrupts.*] No, wait, it was interesting. Can we hear more of it?

EISENSTEIN   Well, I don't think—

BAKHTIN   Yes, please. Put it on again. [EISENSTEIN *plays the record. Billie Holiday's voice, with Lester Young's tenor sax solo in the middle of the song. While the record is playing* EISENSTEIN *takes a drink from the flask.* BAKHTIN *listens very attentively. "All of me, why not take all of me? Can't you see, I'm no good without you?" After a long pause:*] Extraordinary. So this is real jazz music? You know, for a few years I had a neighbor who was a musician, an outstanding clarinetist. He had played with an American Negro band called the Chocolate Babies that toured the Soviet Union in the twenties. Then he had his own Soviet band for a while, but it seems he got into trouble over the repertoire—and ended up in Kustanai, just like me. He was working as a letter carrier. In any case, we became good friends, and he would sometimes tell me about his music. He would always insist that it should be called jazz *music,* not just jazz.

There's a lot of talk about the improvised nature of jazz, but it seems to me that that's mostly just romanticism. There is no such thing as true improvisation. What is interesting about it exists on another level—where jazz music bears a striking similarity to Hellenistic or late medieval literature. It really consists of nothing but a grandiose multiplicity of clichés, quotes, and borrowed phrases—some of those quotations emphasized, others half-hidden, hidden, half-conscious, unconscious, consciously distorted—ironic, tragic, and parodic quotes, references, and cross-references. The boundary between what is original and what belongs to others is fluid, and often intentionally ambiguous. Our modern music—Prokofiev, for example—is based on an overt will to form, a striving, on the composer's part, to subject the entire musical material to his will. Jazz music seems to have the opposite intention. When I listen to that solo—was it a saxophone?—I suddenly understand what my neighbor in Kustanai was talking about: a Copernican music, as opposed to a Ptolemaic one. [*Pause.*] What's the record called?

EISENSTEIN   [*Picks up the record.*] "All of Me," by Marks. [*Chuckles.*] Yes, that's the composer's name: Gerald Marks. Billie Holiday, accompanied by Eddie Heywood and His Orchestra. Tenor saxophone: Lester Young.

BAKHTIN   Young? A paradoxical name for that musician. *Ein Spätgekommener,* as the Germans say. A true melancholic. In jazz music—if I understood that correctly—the instrument often merges with the soloist, his sweaty brow, his gestures, his body movements. But here the opposite is the case: the man disappears into his instrument. The notes merge with the intonation. The reference becomes more important than what is actually played.

EISENSTEIN   Would you like to hear the other side?

BAKHTIN   No. There's really nothing else to say. [*Helps himself to another piece of sausage, takes a hit from the flask. Rolls and lights a cigarette.*]

EISENSTEIN   Jazz interests me because it is film's twin sister. What is it that makes both of them so attractive to the masses? With all due respect, your "contexts of meaning" don't seem to apply here. In both genres there simply is something that *smells* powerful and raw, that speaks to you beyond all enlightened levels of consciousness, *down to the guts,* as jazz musicians put it. And the audience senses that. In film it is the totemic language of images—instead of words, film uses close-ups, visual metaphors, montage. In jazz, of course, it is the monotonous rhythm—the shaman's drum—ethnographers can provide thousands of examples of how rhythm is used to return the congregation to primal, even prenatal states of consciousness. Take this fantastic singer with the boyish name, Billie Holiday. With one leg she stands in a prehistoric, biological, almost botanical world where love is still an unknown concept; with the other, in the cruel capitalist metropolis where love is no longer possible. She spreads her legs, all right, and she does it beautifully.

BAKHTIN   I prefer the saxophone player. Even though those two do reach a remarkable understanding. One could just as well say that she is playing and he is singing. But the lyrics seem embarrassingly sentimental.

EISENSTEIN   Don't be so sure of that. True, the words are horrendous, but the singer takes them and constantly changes them into new utterances—to use one of your expressions. With a smile she wipes off all the sentimentality. With a bent note she opens up an abyss in the idyll. That, too, is a kind of montage. [*Pause.*] I really got this record because the song has acquired a kind of private meaning for me.

BAKHTIN   What is it?

EISENSTEIN   It is—private.

BAKHTIN   [*After a pause.*] I know you're interested in the ecstatic. Surely, jazz music is a superior medium for that? The ecstasy a jazz band can create, within the three-minute format of a gramophone record, is not often equaled by Wagner in five *hours*—no matter how carefully he has greased those slide trombones.

EISENSTEIN   [*Humming to himself.*] "You took the best, so why not take the rest?"

BAKHTIN   *There's* your interpretation.

EISENSTEIN   [*Laughs shrilly.*] Brünhilde singing "All of Me?" Now that's an interpretation they would definitely sack me for! [*Pause.*] No, jazz music won't ever be anything but *Kleinkunst,* no matter how beautiful it is. It'll never reach the heights that interest me.

BAKHTIN   Sometimes the small may contain all of the great. The small genres often give you amazing insights into the great ones' future.

EISENSTEIN   So you think the musical drama of the future will be Wagner in jazz tempo? Yes, they'd really fire me for that kind of interpretation. [*Pause.*] Don't you see? This will be my last engagement. I won't die quite yet; a Gypsy woman promised me that. But a year ago I had never dreamed of being allowed to stage the *Valkyrie,* and in a year's time, I could be hanged for doing it.

[*Pause.*] So what, *che serà, serà.* [*Spreads his hands, looks up at the ceiling, then looks at* BAKHTIN. *Pause.*] You ask me in whose name I speak. [*Gets up, goes to the control panel of the projector. Turns wheels, pushes a few switches. The projector turns slowly, the constellations change. Pause.*] Do you know what this is? The stars above Moscow on Ash Wednesday, 1940. This is what they look like. [*Goes back to* BAKHTIN. *Sits down. In a low voice:*] What is going on is beyond the influence of any human being. It can only be rejected or accepted, and it does not really matter what the response is. The wheel has begun to turn. The Four Horsemen have already passed. Rivers turn in their beds, forests are on the march, animals talk, stones weep, humans eat human flesh. The sun turns dark, the moon reverses its course. Right becomes left, and left becomes right. Faust supervises the building of the White Sea Canal, and Soviet women embroider swastikas on the red flags. Marx's heirs embrace the Führer in Berlin—and I, the Jewish swine Eisenstein, produce Richard Wagner in Moscow. Our country has been transformed into a gigantic high-tension laboratory. One's hand must not shake when the circuit is closed between the poles of regression and progress. The new man will be born! [*Pause.*] Or else, is it really the grand finale, with sets by Hieronymus Bosch? I don't know anymore. But I am willing to bet that if you were a stage director, you couldn't say, No, thanks, either—even if the poster only says the *Valkyrie*, not *Ragnarök.*

BAKHTIN   Fortunately, I don't know anything about the theater. But it is my impression that you, as the director of this performance, will only be allowed to *assist.* Your task will be, more or less, like conducting a record on a turntable. You'll just be making those conjuror's gestures. Come, step down from the conductor's podium. Step down.

EISENSTEIN   I want to find out how far my art can reach. That is the only progress I'm interested in. *Stirb und werde,* right? Through the lowest to the highest. No, even further: through the synthesis of the lowest and the highest to an irresistible form, a form that will include everybody. Everybody! Everybody!! [*Pause. Looks up at the stars.*] Do you think I signed the contract without having read the scenario? Do you think that what is happening is just some goddamned accident?

BAKHTIN [*Coughs.*] Who knows? How many possible combinations do you think the universe contains? Compared to the universe, even Dr. Bauersfeld's fantastic machine is about as crude as a meat grinder. Why do you believe that this, exactly *this,* is the end? There is no end. Have you forgotten what it says in Scripture, the one Giordano Bruno quoted: "What shall be? What has been. What has been? What shall be." There is no center for you to erect your conductor's podium, to build your Tower of Babel. You think the future has arrived. But you've just fallen victim to the dialectical disease. Thesis, antithesis, synthesis—that is the evil trinity! Believe me, in this world the boundary between thesis and antithesis is never a given. It is always in motion: sometimes it disappears entirely, sometimes it reappears behind the back of the thesis, sometimes it runs away from the antithesis. You're in too much of a hurry to reach the synthesis. And that is why you love that sealed endlessness of Wagner's music. The mirror in which everything becomes a revenant; the temple of echoes. But you're just chasing your own tail. You're in too great a hurry. *Omnis festinatio ex parte diaboli est.* There you have the quintessence of it. [*Pause.*] Step down and become one of the chorus, the great chorus that has always existed and will always exist. The chorus Wagner was afraid of. Listen to the silence from the chorus. Become one of the silent. [*Pause.*]

EISENSTEIN Do you know, I would like to make a film with you as the main character. About a man who engages in an endless monologue next to his dead wife's coffin, defends himself, accuses himself, accuses her, falls to his knees, beats her, yes, beats the corpse, hysterically, kisses it, lies to himself, contradicts himself— prosecutor, defendant, witness, and victim all in one person, locked into a speech without end, without a goal, a fiery globe of words that rolls forward without moving an inch, in an eternal *pro et contra,* words, words, words. Yes, a demon of contradiction. The pawnbroker who believes himself to be "a part of the power that always desires evil and always works for the good"—

that would be a part for you, wouldn't it? You do know your Dostoevsky.

No one has come closer to the secrets of the interior mono-logue than he did. He just didn't dare to go all the way. He knew the magic in the convolutions of interior speech, but he stopped at the threshold. The language of film has greater abilities than written language to penetrate the deeps of undifferentiated, pre-logical thought, where all is one and one is all, where the myste-rium of unity has not yet been fractured, the unity of sign and thing, reason and feeling, pain and pleasure, masculine and femi-nine, good and evil.

BAKHTIN   Good and evil? But of course. Beyond good and evil. The superman as pawnbroker. [*Pause.*] No, that's too big a part for me. And besides, I have an infantile phobia of cameras and microphones. But it is true that I have sinned in loquaciousness. Every time I've promised myself to keep my mouth shut, I have started talking again. It doesn't seem possible to stop it. You wanted to discuss Goethe and Wagner, and I started talking about God knows what. No, if I should get a part in a film, it ought to be that detestable sinner Signor Ciapelletto in *The Decameron*. Do you remember the tale? [*Pause.*]

Signor Ciapelletto was the most dyed-in-the-wool scoundrel and cheat northern Italy had ever known. He shortchanged his clients, cheated his workers out of their wages, sweet-talked his creditors, and seduced their wives—and got away with it all due to his ability to talk himself out of just about anything. Neverthe-less, there came a day when he had to make tracks, and he betook himself to Burgundy. There he started all over again, sinning and swindling beyond rhyme or reason. Everything went swim-mingly, but one day this M. Chapelet, alias Signor Ciapelletto, became seriously ill. When he felt that the end was near, he called for a monk to take his confession. And he put everything so cleverly that the monk took him for the most virtuous, right-minded, and humble man who had ever lived in those parts. After Ciapelletto died, the abbot of the monastery, who had been told about his confession, declared that this had been a truly holy man. Soon people started going on pilgrimages to Ciapelletto's grave.

Yes, even miracles happened there, because the people's faith was so strong. As time went on, Signor Ciapelletto, who had deceived everybody with his sinful tongue, was declared a saint.

EISENSTEIN   [*Laughs.*] A great story. [*Pause.*] But it might not work as a film.

BAKHTIN   [*Looks up at the vaulted ceiling.*] It is getting late.

EISENSTEIN   Should we have one last piece?

BAKHTIN   No, thanks. It is Ash Wednesday. The fast has begun.

EISENSTEIN   I meant music.

[BAKHTIN *nods, rolls another cigarette, lights it, while* EISENSTEIN *turns the record over, winds up the gramophone, and lowers the needle. Out of the gramophone emerge, at first scratchily, then with increasing clarity, the strains of Wagner's "The Ride of the Valkyries." Bakhtin exhales a big cloud of smoke.* EISENSTEIN *closes his eyes, beats time with one hand, then lets his hands settle in his lap.* BAKHTIN *gets up quietly and walks away, leaning on his cane, in the direction he initially appeared from. As he passes the candle, it goes out. Music.*]

Notes

In this triptych, questions and persons occur about whose prior careers I have written in other contexts, primarily in my book *Teatern som handling. Sovjetisk avantgardeestetik 1917–1927* [Theater as action. Soviet avant-garde aesthetics 1917–1927] (Stockholm, 1977; 1980.) Here they return in another form and in another historical framework.

The intervals between the dates on which these dialogues are conducted are no less important than the dialogues themselves. Here, as aids to memory, are a few significant dates:

1932   Stalin brings to an end the quarrel between proletarian authors and "fellow travelers" and proclaims national unity.

1933   The Nazis rise to power in Germany.

1934   The First Authors' Congress establishes socialist realism ("socialist in content, popular in form") as the general method to be used by Soviet artists.

1936   Stalin declares that class struggle has ended in the Soviet Union, then starts the Terror.

1939   Germany and the Soviet Union sign a nonaggression treaty. The Communist Party calls a halt to its anti-Fascist propaganda. Germany and the Soviet Union carve up Poland. World War II begins.

1941   Germany attacks the Soviet Union.

Not documentary, the dialogues play with possible significations. However, since human beings themselves are carriers of signification, a few biographical data may be needed.

MIKHAIL BAKHTIN (1889–1975). Philosopher and literary historian. Banished to Siberia in 1928. On his return to Moscow in 1940, he presented his pioneering study of Rabelais (published in 1965), which was, however, not found acceptable as a doctoral dissertation.

BERTOLT BRECHT (1898–1956). German playwright and director, Marxist, in exile 1933–46. Visited the Soviet Union first in 1932, again in 1935, and for a third time in transit to the United States in 1941.

GORDON CRAIG (1872–1966). British theoretician of the theater. Invited by Stanislavski, he staged *Hamlet* in Moscow in 1912.

SERGEI EISENSTEIN (1898–1948). Film director, theoretician of art. Studied with Meyerhold. Spent 1929–32 in Europe, the United States, and Mexico, where he worked on a film that was never finished. His production of the *Valkyrie* premiered at Moscow's Bolshoi Theater on 21 November 1940, in the presence of the German ambassador, and was performed a total of seven times during the 1940–41 season. Eisenstein died in the night between 10–11 February 1948, after he was told to stop shooting his sequel to *Ivan the Terrible.*

PLATON KERZHENTSEV (1881–1940). During the Civil War, the Proletkult movement's leading promoter of plays presenting the revolutionary masses. Later a diplomat and cultural Party Line politician. His article in *Pravda,* "An Alien Theater," 17 December 1937, gave the coup de grâce to Meyerhold's theater.

MEI LAN-FANG (1894–1961). Renewer and prime representative of the classical Chinese theater in our time.

VSYEVOLOD MEYERHOLD (1874–1940). Stage director and actor. Studied with Stanislavski, later on became a radical reformer of the theater. Director of the National Meyerhold Theater 1922–38. Arrested in 1939 as a "spy for the Japanese."

VLADIMIR NEMIROVICH-DANCHENKO (1858–1943). Playwright, stage director. Founder, with Stanislavski, of Moscow's Artistic Theater in 1898; later ousted his colleague from its management.

ERWIN PISCATOR (1893–1966). Stage director, originator of the epic theater. In exile in the Soviet Union 1931–36, later in France and the United States.

ALF SJÖBERG (1903–80). Stage director. One of Sweden's few great international modernists of the theater. Visited the Soviet Union in 1935.

KONSTANTIN STANISLAVSKI (1863–1938). Actor, stage director, teacher. Cofounder of the Artistic Theater. From 1935, director of an opera studio, in which Meyerhold found temporary refuge.

ALEKSANDR TAIROV (1885–1950). Actor, stage director. Founded and was the director of the Chamber Theater from 1914. Died shortly after its closing in 1950.

SERGEI TRETYAKOV (1892–1939). Poet, playwright, reporter. In China 1924–25. In the late twenties, an energetic spokesman for "factual literature." Translated and introduced Brecht to the Soviet Union. Arrested in 1937.

The occult gramophone record played in *Ash Wednesday* needs a commentary. The B-side's "Ride of the Valkyries" may be any recording made in the 1930s. The A-side's "All of Me," however, is Billie Holiday's recording with Eddie Heywood's orchestra. It was made on 21 March (the first day of the astrological year) 1941— hence, *after* the dialogue takes place. Since this is an obvious violation of imaginable chronology—the only one in the triptych—it only seems fitting that the version being played is take C (with a solo by Lester Young that lasts sixteen bars, instead of only eight bars in takes A and B). It was issued for the first time in 1980, in the set *The Lester Young Story,* vol. 5 (Am. Columbia C2 34849).

Stockholm—Munich, February 1987
L. K.